Demon Lover

HELLBOUND
BOOK ONE

HEATHER GUERRE

Preface

Demon Lover touches on topics that may be difficult for some readers, including the death of a parent (off-page, before the story begins), negligent/absent parent, infidelity (perpetrated off-page by a side character), and references to historical enslavement and violence against enslaved people.

"And what hills are those, my love,
those hills so dark and low?"
"Those are the hills of hell, my love,
where you and I must go."

—The Daemon Lover *(c. 1685)*

Chapter One

For the third night in a row, Autumn Havener woke alone in her bed, basking in the afterglow of what had been an incredible sleep-orgasm. Each night had been a different dream, a different dream lover, but the outcome was always the same—a climax so mind-blowing she woke up gasping and writhing.

The first night, she'd dreamt that she'd been captured at sea by a ruggedly handsome pirate and ravished in his quarters belowdecks. For a lawless cutthroat, he'd been surprisingly earnest about consent.

"Do you accept the covenant of fornication?"

"What?" His face seemed to shift, his skin flickering between sun-weathered brawn and unearthly blue.

"Do you agree to this union of flesh?"

Distracted by the mutability of his face, she hadn't quite grasped the question. "'Union of flesh'...?"

The pirate had the temerity to look slightly annoyed with her. Eyes that had previously been brown suddenly gleamed flame blue. "Do you want to fuck me?" he enunciated impatiently.

"Oh. Yes, please."

His features seemed to settle then, locking into the raw-boned, scarred pirate. "You will forget this conversation," he told her before he set to a thorough ravishing.

But she hadn't forgotten. The next night, her dream lover had been a nomadic barbarian king, dressed in animal pelts, wearing a sword. He'd captured her from her peaceful, pastoral village and taken her to his tent as a war prize.

Again, the barbarian king had been unexpectedly concerned about consent, refusing to rip her simple shepherdess's robes off of her quivering body until she'd assured him that she *accepted the covenant of fornication.*

The third night, her subconscious had flipped the script, making Autumn the aggressor. She'd been an evil sorceress who'd captured the golden hero sent to destroy her, and turned him into her helpless sex slave.

"Do you accept the covenant of fornication?" the noble knight asked as she chained him to her bed.

"Dude, what do you think?" She began to unlace his breeches.

"I need you to tell me."

Autumn sighed impatiently. "Yes. I consent. Do you?"

He blinked, taken aback. "What?"

"Do. You. Consent?"

"Do I consent?"

She raised her eyebrows, waiting, her hands poised at the laces of his breeches.

He squinted at her, clearly confused. "Uh. Yes."

"Good. Now look angry. You're my unwilling victim, remember?"

"Right."

Autumn lay in her bed, remembering the way the honorable knight had fought to resist her sorcerous allure. In the end, his body had betrayed him, and he'd succumbed to pleasure as she rode him to her own crashing climax.

The dreams had to be her subconscious's way of telling her that her current dry spell (eighteen months, to the day) had gone on for far too long. The problem was, Autumn wasn't emotionally equipped for casual sex, so she wasn't going to find relief in a hookup. And the shambles of her life meant that she didn't feel like suitable girlfriend material, either. So, until she got her life back on track, it was nothing but her battery-operated boyfriend and filthy dreams.

Thank god for the dreams. They gave her more than a vibrator did, leaving her with the bone-deep satisfaction that came from good sex—the kind of sex usually had with another person. It was probably because they felt so real. Instead of the slowly fading impression of an impossible scenario, the dreams felt more like memories. Savoring the feeling, she drifted back into a dreamless sleep.

～

THE HARSH LIGHT OF MORNING WAS A SOBERING reminder of just how deeply *un*satisfied Autumn was. She sat up, pulling the blankets around her shoulders, and stared bleakly at her surroundings. A year and a half ago, she'd been living in a renovated loft in Chicago's Loop with the man she thought she'd marry, while helping that same man build the company that had turned him from a scruffy, broke grad student into a multi-millionaire.

Somewhere in the five years after meeting each other, Dylan had changed. Instead of the shy, brilliant, kindhearted computer scientist she'd fallen in love with, he'd become an entitled, arrogant prick of a CEO. Entitled enough to think he deserved as many women as he could get, arrogant enough to think she'd forgive him once she found out. He'd been wrong.

Now Autumn lived alone in a spider-infested studio apartment in Back of the Yards. Her only window overlooked an alley crowded with dumpsters. She'd been too proud to keep working at Dylan's company, so instead of managing the visual branding for the fastest growing software company in the United States, she was stuck designing direct mailers for a poorly funded, badly managed non-profit that nobody had ever heard of.

With a sigh, she dragged herself out of bed and started getting dressed for another miserable day at a job she hated with coworkers she could barely tolerate. The Weldon Hope Foundation was ostensibly a charity devoted to funding medical research for genetic birth defects. As a graphic designer, Autumn had no access to the foundation's accounting, but she suspected that things weren't exactly on the up and up with the cashflow. The whole place was so badly managed that its continued operation was somewhat of a mystery. The only rational explanation Autumn could come up with was that the Weldon Hope Foundation was not interested in actually funding anything, and that it only existed as a front for its wealthy founder—Harold Weldon—to illegally shift money around from his various corporate enterprises.

Regardless, after the way things ended with Dylan—loudly and bitterly—she'd had to find a new job without the benefit of a good reference from her last six years of employment. Of all the places she'd applied, interviewed, pleaded, and begged, the Weldon Hope Foundation had been the only one to offer a job.

It's not forever, she told herself, staring dispiritedly in the mirror as she brushed her teeth. Yes, her current workplace was a dysfunctional house of cards, but she was closing in on two years of employment there as the principal designer. If she could stick it out for another year or so, she'd probably be able to jump ship to a much better company, with better pay, and better management.

For now, she had to resign herself to an interminable future spent sharing a windowless office with Bitchy Therese, fixing the endless mistakes of Incompetent Colton, and dodging the persistent flirtation of Creepy Kyle.

At least it was Friday.

Even so, the day went no different than any other.

Therese made a thousand passive-aggressive comments that Autumn pretended not to notice. Colton sent proofs over to the printer that had a major misspelling and some photoshop fuckery that resulted in a stock model with three hands. Kyle cornered her in the break room with an endless monologue about his brother's wife's dad's boat and how maybe someday Autumn would want to go boating with him, he can borrow it any time and they could spend the day on the lake, he'd bet she looked great in a bikini, and they could bring a bunch of sunblock and beer and just... have a good time, *wink*.

The supposed marketing manager—one of Harry Weldon's useless nephews—tended to show up one day a week, and never for the full day. Someone must've threatened to cut off his trust fund, because he was in his office on Monday, constantly calling Autumn in to answer trivial questions that even a stranger off the street could have answered.

At the end of the day, Autumn sat at her desk, listening to her coworkers as they shut down their computers, gathered their things, and left the building. If she lingered at her desk for a little longer, she was less likely to run into Kyle waiting for the train. Within ten minutes, she was entirely alone in the building. All the other employees at the Weldon Hope Foundation left work the exact minute that the clock struck quitting-time. As well they should, Autumn reasoned.

When she'd worked for Dylan, she'd put in hours upon hours of overtime perfecting every microscopic detail of Apollo Technologies' visual presence. In fact, before he'd officially hired her on, Autumn had designed the company logo, vastly improved the website design, and created professional letterhead and business cards—all without receiving a single penny in return. She hadn't expected anything. She'd done it because she cared about his success and believed in his talent. And sure enough, as soon as Dylan implemented her cohesive, crisp designs, things started to take off. Shortly after, Dylan asked her to join the company full-time. With visions of their future as a love-synced power couple, Autumn had happily accepted. And for nearly six years, things had been amazing.

Or so she'd thought. She had no way of knowing how long Dylan's cheating had been going on, or how many other women there'd been. In the eighteen months since Autumn had discovered his infidelity and left him, he'd replaced her in every way. Apollo Technologies had a hotshot new Brand Manager straight out of Harvard Business school. Dylan had an unbelievably beautiful new girlfriend straight out of the pages of Maxim. And Autumn had nothing.

On that depressing thought, she pushed away from her desk and made her way out of the building. The sky was dark, but the city was bright and bustling. Thanksgiving was nearing, and Christmas was little more than a month away. All the holiday cheer seemed like a personal affront to Autumn, who had nothing to celebrate, and nobody to celebrate with.

Friday night stretched ahead of her, empty of plans or company. When Autumn had left Dylan, their friends had—without explicitly saying it—taken his side. After all, he was the genius computer scientist well on his way to becoming a billionaire. Autumn was a nobody with a fine arts degree and a chip on her shoulder.

She returned to her empty apartment with a bag of Thai takeout. In her old life, she would have *never* eaten takeout in bed. But in her current life, her bedroom and her living room were one and the same, and her bed had no choice but to moonlight as a couch. Propping pillows into a comfortable backrest, she turned her TV on and resumed the low-budget sci-fi series she'd been watching over the last couple weeks. She opened her takeout and dug in. Curry and spaceships were as close as she got to happiness these days.

The ugliness of that realization swept away the small measure of contentment she'd managed to find, and she sat in her bed, staring blankly into her takeout container. Bleakness warred with anger until all she was left with was exhaustion. Defeated, she turned off the TV and laid down, pulling the blankets over her head.

"Do you accept the covenant of fornication?"

A handsome, sweaty stablehand loomed over her in the hayloft. The ties on his rumpled tunic had been pulled open, revealing a broad expanse of well-muscled chest. Autumn trailed her fingertips along his collarbone.

"Why do you always ask me that?" She licked the salty taste of his sweat from her fingertips.

The stablehand did a double take. "What?"

"You keep asking. I say yes every time. Can't we just agree that as long as I keep dreaming you up, I'm obviously more than happy to have sex with you?"

"You—you remember me?" His face flickered. Formerly gray eyes gleamed electric blue. Golden skin turned the color of chicory flowers. Faint tattoos wrapped around his throat, disappeared beneath the cover of his tunic.

"I've been a lucid dreamer since I was a kid." She squinted as

the flickering of his features intensified. Tightly cropped brown hair transitioned into shaggy, curling locks of cobalt blue. Long, pointed ears poked out from his hair. Small golden hoops glinted along the edges of his ears. "I can often tell when I'm dreaming—and I always remember my dreams."

His eyes widened with alarm. His grip on her arms tightened. "You're not supposed to remember!" More and more of the golden-skinned stablehand fell away, revealing a monster. Naked, pallid blue skin stretched over a huge frame, ropy with sinewy muscle. Faint tattoos ran over his skin in angular, abstract patterns created from complicated, pointed sigils. Midnight-colored claws curled from his fingertips. His face was broad and hard as an anvil, with a blunt nose and eye-teeth that jutted like small tusks from his lower jaw. A thick, golden hoop pierced his septum. Curling, satyr-like horns protruded from the wild blue tangle of his hair, just above a pair of long, pointed ears. A sinuous tail twitched behind him, catlike in its agitation.

Autumn blinked. "Oh boy," she said uncertainly.

The creature looked down at himself. "What the—" The surrounding hayloft flickered and faded just as the handsome stablehand's features had.

In a few seconds, Autumn was back in her apartment, laying in her own bed, wide awake.

But the creature was still there. The physical reality of his presence was undeniable—she felt the heat of his body, felt his weight pressing her down into her cheap mattress. She stared at his harsh, brutish face, felt the razor touch of his claws on her arms.

A scream rose into her throat—

The monster stared back at her, utterly gobsmacked. Autumn was terrified, but the monster had the stunned look of someone who'd been hit in the head with a mallet. When she finally opened her mouth, instead of screaming, shocked laughter burbled out.

Wild with panic, the monster shoved off of her. "Look away!" he barked, leaping from her bed. He crashed into the nightstand. The lamp, her phone, her stack of books all went crashing to the floor along with the monster's heavy body as he tripped.

Autumn bolted upright, nearly helpless with laughter. "What are you—" she gasped for air. "What the hell are—" She couldn't breathe.

"You've seen nothing! This is a dream!" The monster leapt to his feet and bolted. He only made it one step—the phone cord and the lamp cord were both wrapped around his ankle and they brought him crashing back to the floor like a snared rabbit.

Autumn doubled over, clutching her sides. She couldn't breathe. She was blinded by tears.

"Don't look at me!" the monster roared, covering his face with one claw-tipped hand while the other struggled to disentangle the cords from his ankle.

"You're just—" Autumn gasped for breath, clutching her aching sides. "You're making it—" She doubled over again. Struggling for composure, she hauled in a breath. "You're just getting more tangled," she gasped, grinning like an idiot. She slipped from bed. The monster froze as she approached him. He stared at her from between his fingers. His irises were an unnatural, electric blue, scored with vertical pupils.

Autumn knelt beside his feet and pushed his hand away so that she could unravel the cords. His feet were paw-like, with his weight borne on claw-tipped toes, while the rest of the foot arched upwards towards a backward-pointing hock. Unlike animal paws, though, his strange blue skin was as smooth as human skin.

It took Autumn a few seconds to untangle the cords. Her laughter subsided to slightly hysterical giggles. By the time she freed him, she'd gotten her breath back. She sat back, clicked the lamp on, and looked at the bizarre creature.

He was composed entirely of shades of blue, ranging from the midnight color of his claws and horns, to the cobalt of his hair, to the ashy cerulean of his skin. Golden piercings winked against the blue—small hoops in his ears, a thicker hoop in septum of his nose, pointed barbells through his nipples. A jagged, blue-black scar ran across his throat from ear to ear. The tattooed lines and runes that ran over his skin seemed to pulse softly with a faint glow. Cobalt hair furred his chest and drew a narrow line down his torso, leading straight to a majestically endowed, human-looking cock, for all that it was blue.

She'd been staring at his dick for too long, Autumn realized with a start. She tore her gaze back to his face. He'd lowered his hand and was staring at her with a frown that drew his cobalt eyebrows together, giving her the same searching assessment she'd done on him.

There wasn't much to see. Autumn was not the kind of woman who turned heads, but neither was she the kind who invited ridicule. She was dark-eyed and dark-haired. Her skin was smooth and even, but had the pallor of someone who spent all her daylight hours under fluorescent lighting, along with perpetual shadows beneath her eyes. She was a woman of average height and average weight, with a tidy waist, but the kind of voluptuous hips that made buying jeans incredibly frustrating. Her breasts were small, but nicely shaped. Her sable hair was thick and long, but also frizzy and entirely resistant to styling. She wasn't unhappy with her appearance, but she wasn't particularly thrilled by it either.

Grateful for the cover of her nightshirt, she tugged it low to cover her thighs. "So..." she said, fiddling with the cords. "You want to tell me what the hell is going on?"

The monster's expression blanked. He shifted his weight to a more dignified sitting position.

"You're having a dream."

"I know that I'm not."

His frown was back. "Then why aren't you screaming?"

"I was going to," she admitted. "But you looked so scared— even though *I'm* the one who should be scared." A residual giggle bubbled out of her. "And, honestly, my life is such shit right now. Being dragged to Hell by the demon under my bed might actually be an improvement."

His frown shifted from confusion to affront. "That's not what I do."

"No?" She leaned back, resting against her bed. "What do you do then?"

"I—uh..." he looked away from her. His face darkened, a purple flush suffusing his cheeks. Good lord, was the monster *blushing*?

"Come on. I woke up in the middle of the night with you on top of me. You owe me an answer." Not for the first time, it occurred to Autumn that she should be absolutely terrified. But despite his monstrous appearance, the creature looked so flustered and uncomfortable that she almost started laughing again.

"I'm an incubus," he muttered, his voice a low growl.

Autumn was taken aback. "Did you say an *incubus*?"

He nodded, still not meeting her eyes.

She sputtered. "Were you—were we—*actual sex*?" Given a second to think, she might've come to that conclusion on her own.

"Yes." The incubus's flush deepened. "But only by your consent."

Do you accept the covenant of fornication? echoed in her

mind, along with her own impatient replies. *I need you to tell me*, he'd insisted.

"Okay..." Autumn stared at him. She didn't know where to go from here. After a moment, he seemed to gain the nerve to look up at her. His lips were pressed into a tense line, the tips of his lower canines overlapping his upper lip. His unnaturally blue eyes were shadowed with uncertainty as he searched her face.

"So," Autumn broke the tense silence. "An incubus. A sex demon, right?"

He nodded, still watching her with cautious eyes. His tail lay in his lap, and he fiddled with it nervously.

"What exactly does that mean, then?"

The incubus hesitated. He seemed to need a second to work up his nerve. "I'm sustained by sexual energy. I'm summoned by the desire of those who have an abundance of unfulfilled—"

"Okay, yep. Got it," Autumn said quickly. It was her turn to blush and look away. She was so hard up for it that she'd somehow hired herself a supernatural gigolo. "Uh. So. What happens now?"

"I could try to put you back into a dream state, but I don't know if it would work. I've never had a hostess awake from the dream. Or remember me. Or..." he trailed off, then shook his head abruptly as if clearing it. "I could just...well, the thing is, you're still radiating a great deal of sexual energy and if I don't harvest a little bit of it... uh. Well. Without harvesting from you, I'll dissipate."

"Dissipate?"

"The energy that compels my physical form will run out, and I will simply... cease to exist."

"Are you telling me you will *die* without sex?"

"Well, to be more precise, I can only harvest your sexual energy through orgasm. So, it's not sex so much as it's your pleasure." He took a breath and straightened his shoulders, steeling himself for something. "So, if you wouldn't mind? I can be quick about it."

Autumn stared at him. "*You* will die if *I* don't have an orgasm?"

He nodded. The end of his tail flicked in his lap. He clutched it in a white-knuckled hand.

"Can't you find some other lonely, sex-starved sad sack?"

"I was summoned by *your* need. I can't leave you until you release me."

"Oh. Uh..." Autumn sat back. "Then I release you." She waved her hands vaguely. "Be free."

For the first time, the incubus's posture eased, and his mouth softened from that hard line, revealing a full, firm lips curved into a rueful smile. "It doesn't work that way. Your need summoned me. I will only be released when you no longer need me."

"How does that happen?"

The demon shrugged, a surprisingly human gesture. "I've never been in a position to know. As soon as I'm no longer needed by one hostess, I'm summoned to another."

Autumn frowned. "Is that all you do, then? You just... fuck?"

The demon went back to fiddling with his tail. "No. I come to this world at sundown every night. I have to wait for my hostess to enter a dream state. Once I harvest an orgasm, I leave her to sleep, and I can do whatever I like."

"What do you like to do?"

He gestured at himself. "I can't exactly mingle among humans. I go to quiet, empty places, where I won't be seen."

Autumn felt a sad little pang in her heart. "Don't you get lonely?"

He shrugged again, looking down at his tail. "In the

summer it's not so bad. If there's a street festival going on, I can sit on a rooftop and watch. It's a lot easier to keep hidden in a crowd, in the dark."

The sadness intensified. "What do you do in the daylight? Do you sleep?"

"I've never seen daylight, nor do I sleep. Incubi are night demons and demons do not sleep."

Autumn frowned. "So, what do you do during the day?"

"I am recalled to the Underworld." There was a foreboding quality to his words that made Autumn shiver.

"What's that like?"

He lifted his gaze to hers, eyes bleak. "Pray you never find out."

"Should I start going to church?" she asked nervously.

The demon waved a clawed hand scornfully. "*Religion*," he scoffed.

An uncomfortable silence lapsed between them. They regarded each other warily. After a moment, Autumn got to her feet. The demon hurried to follow.

"So..." she skirted around him, going to the narrow galley kitchen to pour a glass of water. "How is this going to work, then? Do I need to fall back asleep so you can... do your thing?"

"That would probably be easiest for you. If you're in a dream state, I can appear human to you—like somebody you'd be attracted to."

Autumn's knee-jerk response was to insist that he was perfectly attractive, but her gaze was caught by the end of his tail, held in his blue-skinned, clawed hands. She lifted her eyes to his face, with those jutting canine teeth and eerie, snake-like eyes. "Um. Sure. The only problem is, I'm going to have a hell of a time falling asleep now that I know you're here, especially with the anticipation of what's going to happen once I do."

"Do you have a sleeping drug? I know many humans use them."

Autumn shook her head. Usually she had the opposite problem—she was tired all the time. She often felt fully capable of falling asleep while sitting upright at her desk. But right now, adrenaline and anxiety had her feeling wide-awake.

"I could...perhaps if you're tense... a massage?"

She looked at his hands, envisioned those razor claws sliding over her skin, and shivered. "Um... no, that's alright."

The incubus nodded stiffly. His face was flushed again, his cheeks purple. For a sex demon, he was not exactly a maestro at the whole seduction thing.

"Are you sort of new at this?" Autumn asked gently.

The demon frowned at her. His pointed ears flicked back like an angry horse. "*No,*" he said frostily. "However, I've always appeared to my hostesses in a body and scenario that they desired. This current situation is totally irregular, and as soon as I return to the Underworld, you can rest assured that I will—"

Autumn held her hands up in surrender. "Sorry, sorry. I wasn't insulting your competence. You just seem so uncomfortable." She glanced at the glass of water in her hands. "Would you like something to drink?"

"No, thank you," he said, still clearly miffed.

Autumn leaned against the counter, finishing her water and thinking. "I know," she said, putting the empty glass in the sink. "Allergy pills always knock me out. I'll go take some."

She returned from the bathroom with two little antihistamine capsules in hand and washed them down with another glass of water. The demon busied himself by righting her end table and putting her things back on it. Autumn quirked a little smile. He might not be a smooth operator, but he was not a bad guy for a demon. She'd met worse humans.

"Alright. So, I'll just lay down?" Autumn slid into bed.

The demon stood awkwardly beside the bed, watching her.

"Could you maybe not loom over me? You can sit." She gestured at the little red armchair beside her dresser.

"Yes, of course."

When he was settled in the chair, Autumn turned off her lamp. The room plunged into darkness, and for a minute, she couldn't see anything. But then her eyes adjusted, and she saw his big, horned silhouette sitting stiffly in the chair.

She closed her eyes and tried to fall asleep. Her mind was racing, but it wasn't long before the antihistamine kicked in, and her thoughts slowed. She yawned, shifting in bed. One last important though crossed her mind.

"Hey, uh—"

"Yes?" The incubus asked politely.

"What's your name?"

He didn't answer.

"Are you still there?"

"Yes, I'm here," he said. His deep, baritone voice sounded odd.

"Do you not want me to know?"

Another beat of silence. At last, he said, "You may call me Irdu."

"Irdu," she repeated sleepily. "I'm Autumn."

"I know," he said in a low voice. "Go to sleep."

"Okay. Goodnight Irdu. See you soon."

And with that, she drifted away.

$$Chapter\ Two$$

He appeared as an ordinary man—human colored, and without horns, fangs, or claws—laying with her in a cabana on a tropical beach. Gauzy white curtains fluttered in the breeze. The sound of the waves shushed over the sand. He leaned over her, cupping her face with one hand. His lips were a hair's breadth from hers as he whispered, "Do you accept the covenant of fornication?"

"Irdu?"

He huffed impatiently, leaning back. "Yes. Now, tell me—do you accept the covenant of fornication?"

Autumn searched his handsome new face. He had short black hair, swarthy skin, and warm brown eyes. She took his hand and examined the blunt fingertips. She ran her finger over the smooth edges of his fingernails. When she looked back up at him, his eyes flickered to electric blue.

"This feels weird now that I know what you really look like." She traced her fingertips along the line of his jaw. Beneath her touch, human skin faded to demonic blue. "I feel like I'm making you put a bag over your head."

He caught her hand, pulling it away from his face. "Stop that. You're breaking the dream state again."

"Sorry."

"It's fine. Just answer me—do you accept the covenant of fornication?"

"Yes."

The flickering instability of the dream state seemed to settle. Irdu looked completely human as he cupped her face again and brought his lips to hers in a tender kiss. Autumn tried to relax into the kiss, but she couldn't stop opening her eyes to peer at the handsome, human face and try to reconcile those features with the blue-skinned demon.

"What are you doing?" Irdu's lips moved over hers, his tone more than a little annoyed.

"I don't know if this is going to work."

Irdu pulled back. He looked down at her, brow furrowed. "Would you prefer if I looked different?"

His human features flickered and faded. Around them, the cabana dissolved.

They were on Autumn's bed, Irdu's big, strange body poised over hers. His harsh features looked oddly endearing with a perplexed frown. Moonlight streamed through her window, illuminating everything with a silvery glow.

Irdu looked up at their surroundings and growled in frustration. "You broke the dream state again!"

Autumn slid back, raising herself up on her elbows. "Sorry." She chewed her lip. She was the one who'd summoned Irdu, whether intentionally or not. And now, he was dependent on her for his survival. But slipping into dreamland wasn't going to work—not when she knew it wasn't real. "What if we just forgot about the dream thing?"

Irdu sat back on his haunches, putting distance between them. "I can't change my appearance if you're awake."

"That's probably better."

He stared at her. "You would—you would have me like *this?*" He gestured skeptically at his body.

Autumn let her eyes roam over him—blue skin, fangs, claws, tail, and all. She nodded. "It's not like I don't already know what you look like now."

Irdu remained where he was, watching her with a wary expression.

"Is that okay?" Autumn asked gently.

"I've never served a hostess this way—as myself." He was back to plucking fretfully at his tail, but he didn't look away from her.

"Well, I can try to go back to sleep," Autumn said, checking the time on her phone. "But sunrise is only three hours away."

Irdu nodded, looking a little stupefied. "You would really have me in this form? You aren't revolted?"

Autumn sensed that he needed a sincere answer, so she sat up, taking her time to consider him. Despite all his peculiarities, he wasn't revolting. He was big and muscular, with broad shoulders and strong arms. The tattoos that covered his body only highlighted the peaks and valleys of those muscles. Despite the craggy harshness of his face, he had lovely lips and striking eyes. They were such a bright blue, they seemed to glow from within. And then there was his cock. It was a perfectly shaped marvel of phallic beauty. Even in its relaxed state, it was long and thick. Autumn wondered what it would feel like in her hand. And her mouth. And her—

A faint blush heated her cheeks. "No," she told him honestly. "I'm not revolted. You may not be human, but you're still a man. And besides, human women have a long tradition of wanting to get it on with inhuman creatures—werewolves, vampires, cursed princes, tentacle monsters, the minotaur... the list goes on." As a teenager she'd had a thing specifically for gargoyles, thanks to an animated series she had been addicted to.

Irdu seemed to relax somewhat. "Yes. I've had hostesses who..." he trailed off, glancing at Autumn guiltily.

She laughed. "Never had to talk to one of us about your previous lays? Don't worry, I'm not offended."

"Well." he glanced out her window, at the darkness of the sky. "Er... shall we?"

Autumn laughed again, this time nervously. "Okay."

Irdu crawled forward cautiously, his expression uncertain. He stopped just in front of Autumn, searching her face as if waiting for her to recoil.

Instead, she leaned forward, closing the distance between them, and cupped his cheek. He froze at her touch. "Could you —I mean, would it be alright if I... uh, explored you, a little bit? Just to get comfortable?"

"Of course," Irdu said, sounding just as unnerved as she was. "Should I sit here, or...?"

"Could you lay down on your back? Will that bother your tail?"

"I can do that."

Autumn moved over so that he could ease onto his back in the middle of her bed.

"Is there anywhere you don't like to be touched?"

Irdu glanced up at her, looking as though he wasn't sure if she was serious or not. He seemed to realize that she was. "You can touch me anywhere."

"Okay." She let out an embarrassed little huff. "Just tell me if you don't like what I'm—"

"Touch me anywhere it pleases you, Hostess."

Autumn grimaced. "*Blegch*. Call me Autumn."

He looked uncertain. "That's not really—"

"Please?"

He huffed. "Alright then. *Autumn.*"

She smiled. "Can I touch your tail, Irdu?"

His eyes widened at the sound of his name. "Of course," he said faintly.

He lifted his hips and slid his tail out. The end was tufted like a lion's, with the same cobalt hair that grew on his head and chest and that arrowed down to frame that intimidating blue cock. *Let's not get ahead of ourselves.* Autumn caught the end of his tail and ran her fingers through the tuft. Irdu laid stiffly, watching her with poorly concealed unease.

"Are you sure this is okay? You seem really uncomfortable." She dropped his tail.

"No, no. It's fine." He lifted the tip of his tail, draping it back in her hands. "It's just that I'm not usually the passive one in these encounters. It is very odd to simply lay here. I feel I should be doing something for you."

She smoothed the tuft again. "You *are* doing something for me—you're letting me explore you." She lay his tail down and edged closer to his body. He laid calmly, but Autumn could still see a little reticence in his eyes. "Can I touch your horns?"

He nodded.

Autumn slid astride his torso. She was still wearing the t-shirt and underwear that she usually slept in, but the heat of his naked skin seeped through the thin fabric, warming her intimately. She squeezed her thighs compulsively, gripping his body. Irdu's big hands came to rest on her hips. She felt the faint prick of each claw against her skin and shivered—and it wasn't a bad shiver.

Irdu's gaze flashed to hers. His slitted pupils dilated wide until his whole eye was consumed by black. Autumn gasped and froze.

"I'm sorry," Irdu said hoarsely. "I'm sorry, when I feel your arousal, I react. My eyes…"

"Shh, it's fine. I was just surprised." She wiggled a little, adjusting her seat. The friction on her core was just what she needed. Warmth kindled low in her belly. Irdu's grip tightened on her hips. His claws bit into her skin, sending delicious tension coursing through her.

Irdu let out a shaky breath. Though they were entirely black, Autumn could tell his eyes were searching her face. "You are truly reacting to *me*? Like *this*?"

Autumn smiled lazily. "Sure seems like it." Feeling more confident, she leaned forward, bracing one hand on the mattress and reaching out with the other to stroke the curve of one of his horns. "Does that feel like anything for you?"

"I'm not a human man, Hostess—"

Her arousal dampened. "*Ugh*. Autumn, please."

"*Autumn*," he corrected himself hurriedly. "I'm sorry—Autumn. *Autumn*." Each iteration of her name was more intense, bordering on desperate.

"I like when you say my name," she told him.

"I know. I can feel it. I was trying to tell you, I'm not a human man. Your touches don't inflame me the way human men feel desire. I draw my pleasure from yours. Whatever gives you the greatest pleasure will give me the greatest pleasure."

"Really?" Feeling bold, Autumn reached out so that she was holding both his horns. "So, if I used your horns to steer you while you—" Her words died on a surge of arousal.

"*Yes*," Irdu said hoarsely. "*Yes*, Autumn. Please, use me, take what you need."

Her grip tightened on his horns as she rocked her sensitized sex against his torso. Each press sent a lovely bolt of pleasure through her. And with each bolt of pleasure, Irdu groaned and writhed beneath her, his fingers and claws digging harder into her hips.

"Come here," Irdu urged, pulling her hips towards his face. "Let me taste you."

"How do you know exactly what I want?" Autumn gasped, sliding forward.

"I can't read your mind, if that's what you're asking." Irdu took one hand from her hips, reaching over to hook a claw in her panties. "But I can feel what arouses you, and I can guess what would make it even better." He slid her panties to the side, and his obsidian gaze fixed on her bared flesh with undisguised hunger. "Come here, Autumn," he growled.

Still gripping his horns, she inched forward until she was kneeling on either side of his head, her shins pressed against his shoulders. Irdu lifted his head and traced his tongue along the seam of her sex. Fierce pleasure lanced through her, nearly debilitating in its intensity. They both groaned, curling towards each other like matching bookends.

"Good?" Irdu asked, panting.

She grinned unsteadily at him. "You know it is."

"Then come back here." With one hand, he hoisted her forward until she was seated fully on his face. His mouth opened and his tongue stroked into her, plunging into her core.

"*Ah!* Irdu!" She pulled on his horns, rolling her hips to ride his mouth. She felt the press of his fangs, and instead of alarming her, it only made her hotter, needier. His liquid black eyes watched her intently as he devoured her. He growled his pleasure against her wet, swollen flesh. His claws bit into her skin, a delicious pain.

She gasped and sobbed with each devouring stroke of his tongue, gripping his horns to steer his head exactly where she wanted him, mercilessly riding his hungry, pleasing mouth. Her thighs clamped tight on his head as the pleasure sharpened and accelerated, coursing through her body, pulling every muscle tight. She met his gaze, black and inhuman, but stark with the same desperate need that she felt—and she exploded.

Unaware of anything but the mindless pleasure wracking her body, she arched and bucked, rocked by wave after wave of obliterating ecstasy. It went on forever, a helpless, electric dance. She heard drumbeats and saw firelight flickering on cave walls. She felt the pull of the moon, heard the hum of the stars. She turned into wind and whispered away into the night. Endless darkness surrounded her.

In slow degrees, she slipped back into her body. First she felt her heart pounding, her blood pulsing. Then her lungs, gusting like bellows. Then her skin, damp with sweat, tingling with pleasured aftershocks. Then the warm mass of the body beneath hers, all hard flesh and hot skin.

Irdu, she mouthed on a voiceless breath. She realized she was still sitting on his face and crawled clumsily off of him, dropping beside him on the bed.

"Sorry," she said breathlessly. "I hope I didn't suffocate you."

Irdu said nothing. She turned to look at him, and found him staring dazedly at the ceiling, his hands still frozen into the positions they'd been in—holding her hips with one and her panties aside with the other. His eyes were no longer solid black, but dancing with electric blue. It was like watching the aurora borealis through two small windows.

"Irdu?"

"Give me a second," he said hoarsely, hands dropping limply to his chest.

Autumn grinned and huddled against him, stroking a hand over the downy fur on his chest. She glanced down his body. Despite his apparent gratification, he was soft.

"Do you get hard?" she asked.

"Only if you need me to," he said, breathing a little more steadily now.

"Do you ejaculate?"

"No. In a dream state, I can give the illusion of it, if you enjoy that feeling."

She shook her head and laid her head on his shoulder, still stroking his chest. "I don't want an illusion."

"I can't believe you—" he hauled in an unsteady breath. "I've never—" He dragged a hand over his face, still breathing jaggedly.

She hid her smile by pressing her face against him. "I was your first, huh?"

"Yes," he said, sounding stunned. "You're the first hostess who's ever come because of *me*—the real me."

It occurred to Autumn that, while she was cuddled up against Irdu, he was simply laying passively beside her. He was an incubus, she reminded herself, a sex demon. Not a romance demon—not a cuddle demon. Self-conscious, she eased away from him.

"So, now what? Do you usually just leave once you get what you need?" she asked.

"Oh." Irdu sat up. The lovely aurora effect faded from his eyes until they were back to being electric-blue snake eyes. He looked away from her. "Yes, of course. I can—"

"No, wait." Autumn lunged, catching his arm before he could teleport back to Hell or whatever he was planning. "I didn't mean I wanted you to leave. I just didn't—" she floundered for words. "I don't know. This is kind of a strange situation for me."

"And for me," Irdu assured her. "Would you like me to stay?"

"If you don't want to, I don't want to make you."

"Would you like me to stay until you fall asleep?"

Autumn looked down at her hands. *Yes.* When she looked up, Irdu had closed the distance between them, peering intently at her.

"Tell me what you want, Hostess."

"Autumn!" she growled.

"Autumn. Autumn. Autumn," he repeated to himself. He looked back at her. "Tell me what you want, Autumn. I exist for your pleasure."

"That's—wow. That's a lot of pressure."

"Is it?"

"Yeah."

He regarded her for a moment. "Most would see it as having a lot of power. You can use me however you wish."

Autumn grimaced. "I don't want power over you. I want you to feel as good as you make me feel."

Irdu's smile began small, incredulous. He gazed at her, his eyes softening. His smile grew slowly, revealing those monstrous fangs in all their glory. She remembered the press of them against her most intimate flesh and flushed with delicious heat. But after the orgasm she'd just had, she was as wrung out as an old rag. She still hadn't totally gotten her breath back.

"I *do* feel as good as you, Autumn. Tell me what would please you best. Should I stay, or go?"

"Stay, please? Just until I fall asleep?"

His smile turned gentle. "I can do that. In the chair?" He nodded at the chair in which he'd waited for her to fall asleep.

"No, stay in bed. Would you hold me?" she asked, her entire face going crimson. She'd never had to *ask* a man to cuddle with her after sex.

"You want to be held by me?" He glanced down at his demon body.

"Is that okay?"

"Of course." Irdu slid closer to her, easing onto his side.

Autumn curled against him, pulling the blanket over them both. His arm curved around her back, holding her snugly against him. "Is this alright?" he asked.

"That's good," she murmured, feeling the drugging pull of overdue sleep.

"You know, I've never done this before, either."

"Cuddled?"

"That. And I've never stayed the night with a hostess."

Autumn slid an arm across his broad torso, holding tight to him. "Do you like it?" she asked.

"It's...very nice." He sounded uncertain, a little bemused.

"Good," she murmured, slipping inexorably into unconsciousness.

Chapter Three

Saturday morning dawned gray and cold, but Autumn woke feeling golden and warm. She stretched lazily, blinking and yawning and looking around her dingy, spider-infested studio with a less critical eye. She sat up, snugging herself in her blankets, feeling happy and sated, but with no idea why.

As her brain booted up into full wakefulness, last night returned to her in a surge. With a gasp, she threw her blankets off and leaped out of the bed. Last night could *not* have been real. But it felt real. It felt like a memory, not a dream. She stared at the bed, as if she could divine meaning from the rumpled sheets and smushed pillows.

Demons weren't real. Awkward, generous sex demons were *definitely* not real. And yet...

Autumn went to the bathroom, intending to wash her face and brush her teeth, hoping the cleansing might clear her mind a bit. But as she passed the mirror above her sink, a flash of color caught her eye. She froze, staring at her reflection. High on her hip, livid red claw marks scored her skin. Deep red points where they'd punctured her, and long sweeping lines where they'd dragged over her skin

Awed, she touched them gingerly, and was rewarded with a pulse of tenderness. Rough, wounded skin abraded her fingertips.

Real.

Last night was real.

He was real.

Did that mean he was coming back tonight? He'd said he needed to get an orgasm from her every night. But he'd also told her that once he fulfilled *her* needs, he'd move on to someone else. Autumn's heart dropped into her stomach. Last night hadn't just met her needs—he'd exceeded them.

No! she thought plaintively. She wanted to see him again. Not just because of the mind-blowing orgasm he'd given her—the likes of which she'd never experienced before—but also because he was kind of funny, and sweet, and she wanted to know more about his weird life.

She usually spent Saturday running errands, cleaning her tiny apartment, and then vegetating in front of her television. Sometimes she went out with the two remaining friends she had—the ones who hadn't decided that a relationship with Dylan was more profitable than pesky things like having principles. But those two friends, Marcus and Liz, happened to be married to each other, and had recently had a baby. They had more important things to do than entertain a miserable shut-in.

Three times, Autumn checked the time of the sunset, then glanced impatiently at the clock. Would Irdu appear as soon as the sun went down? Would he appear at all? What if, after delivering an orgasm that still had her questioning reality, he'd served out his term with her, and had moved on?

. . .

THE SUN SET AT PRECISELY 4:24 P.M. AUTUMN SAT AT the end of her bed. She'd been trying to distract herself by watching TV, but couldn't focus on the screen. Eventually, she'd given up, turning the TV off and sitting in nervous silence as the sun dipped lower towards the horizon. When the last few rays of sunlight faded from the sky, Autumn turned away from her window, breathlessly waiting.

But he didn't show.

Autumn waited. An hour passed, and still no Irdu. Another hour passed, and another, and another. When midnight rolled around, Autumn had to accept that she wasn't going to see him again.

It wasn't fair to feel abandoned—after all, he had no choice in the matter. But regardless, she felt an ache in her chest not terribly unlike the ache she felt when she'd discovered Dylan's infidelity. She crawled into bed, pulled the covers over her head, and closed her eyes against the self-pitying tears.

*"D*O *YOU ACCEPT THE COVENANT OF FORNICATION?"*

Autumn blinked. "What's this?"

The handsome street thief frowned, puzzled. Behind him, the gold-capped domes of the palace gleamed in the moonlight. The two of them were alone, high above the city in an empty minaret. Autumn was still wearing the shackles from the slave-auction he'd rescued her from. This was the part where she was meant to demonstrate her gratitude, but she found herself feeling more angry than anything.

"What do you mean?" he asked. "You built this fantasy yourself. It's evolved quite a bit over the last twenty years, but I believe it started when you were young, and you saw—"

"I thought you weren't coming back!" To her mortification, she felt hot tears welling in her eyes.

"You—what?" The street thief's features flickered, warm brown skin giving way to sigil-marked blue. "Why would you think that?"

"Because, you said—" Her throat was impossibly tight. She couldn't speak at all. She pulled her legs to her chest and buried her face against her knees. A moment later, she felt a light touch on her back.

She looked up, and they were back in her room, on her bed. Irdu looked like he was supposed to, his electric blue eyes peering fretfully into hers.

"I'm sorry, I don't know what I did wrong." His touch on her back was hesitant, his elbow crooked awkwardly, as if he weren't certain how to comfort someone. "I didn't detect any emotional negativity attached to that fantasy. I can try something else. What would you like?"

Autumn wiped her cheeks. "I told you yesterday, I don't want an illusion."

Irdu frowned at her. "I don't understand. Yesterday was unusual, but surely you don't want—"

"Yes," she cut him off. "That's what I want. I told you—I already know what you look like. The illusions feel wrong."

"You want...*this?*" He gestured to himself skeptically.

Clearly words weren't getting through to him. Autumn threw her arms around his neck. He stiffened in surprise, pulling back from her, but she held on and pressed a kiss to his lips. She felt his fangs against her mouth. Warmth kindled low in her belly

Irdu pulled back from her, wide-eyed. Those narrow, snake-like pupils searched her face. "Really?" he asked

Autumn nodded. She eased against him until she was in his lap, every inch of her body pressed against his. She could feel his muscular heat through her thin cotton nightshirt, feel the hard press of his chest against the soft weight of her sensitive breasts.

Arousal simmered gently through her. Irdu shuddered, and his pupils dilated until the whole of his eyes were black. Those fathomless black depths fixed on her mouth. He leaned into her—

"Where were you?" she asked softly.

"What?"

"The sun went down a little before four-thirty. Why didn't you come to me?"

Irdu stared at her. The black receded from his eyes until the blue irises were back. Narrow elliptical pupils looked into hers. "I was waiting for you to fall asleep."

"Tomorrow, you can come here right away. I mean, if you want to."

"You would want me here that soon?"

"Yes."

Irdu was quiet, thinking. After a moment's consideration, he nodded. "You'd prefer to get it out the way, I suppose. That's reasonable. I should have asked. But I never would have been able to guess that you'd want to do this outside of the dream state again. Perhaps if I'd known that—"

"We don't have to 'get it out of the way.' You could just... hang out."

"Hang out?" he repeated incredulously.

Autumn felt heat crawling up the back of her neck. "Sorry. You don't have to. I just thought maybe you'd—"

Irdu leaned forward, silencing her with the softest of kisses. There was no heat, no sensuality behind it. It was a gentle touch of innocent affection. "You are the most unusual hostess I've ever had."

"Well, you're the most unusual lover I've ever had."

"Lover?" he repeated wonderingly. He smiled, revealing even, pointed teeth bookended with a predator's gleaming canines. Autumn bit her lip and smiled back.

"Um, so, are you... 'hungry,' or whatever you call it? I don't want you to be uncomfortable. We can—"

"Don't worry yourself over that. I don't feel hunger. I won't feel any lack until I'm recalled to the Underworld. Passing through the portal will disincorporate me if I haven't harvested enough energy."

"Why go back, then?"

"I have no choice."

"Are you a prisoner?"

He didn't answer.

Autumn pulled back from their embrace to look at him. "Are you?"

He wouldn't meet her eyes. "In a manner of speaking."

"Is it possible to escape?"

His gaze flicked to hers. "No," he said. But Autumn hadn't missed the briefest hesitation before he answered. He was lying to her for some reason.

For now, she decided not to press it. "Well, if you want to just relax for a little bit instead of being my on-demand sex dispenser, we could watch TV. I'm sort of addicted to this really bad sci-fi show. It's terrible, but I can't stop watching it. I need somebody else to watch it so they can agree with me about how terrible it is."

Irdu had an odd look on his face. "I've seen quite a lot of television in my time, but I never intentionally watched something I didn't enjoy."

"Oh, well, we can do something else." She tried to think of an alternative that would appeal to him. "We could play cards?" Autumn was acutely aware that her own pathetic loneliness was driving her to force Irdu into a friendship that he may not actually want. But she was too needy to stop herself. And Irdu had told her that he didn't have anything to do after he was done with her, so maybe he wouldn't mind so much.

He was watching her now, that odd expression still on his face. She couldn't read him—that expression could be anything from pity, to amusement, to disdain.

"...or not. If you just want to—"

Irdu pulled away from her, and her heart sank into her stomach. "Go on then," he said, gesturing towards the TV. "Show me your terrible television program."

Autumn's heart jumped back up, and she couldn't stop the manic smile from spreading over her face. She turned away from him, hiding her pleasure as she fiddled with the TV remote.

"You watch a lot of television? What do you watch?"

"News programs and documentary films. I try to keep up with the happenings in the world. I like to see how real people are living, how they interact with each other." He paused. "And... I like shows with a lot of people. People being together."

There was something heartbreaking about that, but Autumn kept her expression neutral. "Well, this one has a lot of people together." She crawled back to the headboard, arranging pillows and blankets into a comfortable backrest. Irdu watched her, remaining at the foot of the bed. She settled herself on one side of the bed and gestured for Irdu to take the open space beside her.

He crawled over, and Autumn was struck anew by the oddness of everything about him. How many times had she seen Dylan do the same—crawl across the bed to join her? Now she was seeing an entirely new man do it, but this man had claws and horns and blue skin and a tail and strange paw-like feet. She realized, in the low light, that the sigils on his skin gave off a faint, wavering glow. His tail flicked to the side as he settled to sit next to Autumn. She stared at it for a second before remembering herself and flipped the blanket over their legs.

"Okay, so all you need to know is that this is set in an imaginary future in New York City where aliens have landed and are secretly infiltrating human society," she told him.

"I've been in New York," Irdu said. He was sitting rigidly, as if her bed were made of nails. "Several generations ago, I think. There were no automobiles then. Women were still wearing corsets."

Autumn was silent for a moment, considering the image of a pre-Edwardian woman welcoming the attentions of an incubus, and felt an unwarranted stab of jealousy. Except that wasn't precisely what had happened, she reminded herself. That woman in New York, all those years ago, would've simply believed she was having some *amazing* dreams. Autumn was the only one to have ever known what Irdu really was.

Placated, she asked, "Where else have you been?"

"Many, *many* places. Too many to list. A lot of them had different names than they do now. Some of them no longer exist." He answered readily, but his posture remained stiff, his gaze pinned on the TV screen.

"How old are you?"

He hesitated. "I don't entirely know. I..." he thought back for a moment. "I witnessed the construction of the Tower of Babel."

"The Tower of Babel is *real?*"

"It was called Eurmeiminanki by the people who built it. It was a ziggurat in Borsippa."

"Did it really have anything to do with languages changing?" Autumn asked, knowing it was a silly question.

He smiled at her sheepishness. "No. The workers already spoke many different languages. They were slaves, captured from other regions in war."

"So the tower's construction wasn't stopped by an angry god?" It wasn't an entirely facetious question, considering that she was speaking to an actual, legitimate demon.

"I can't answer that with any certainty," he answered sincerely. "But construction halted when the slaves rebelled."

"What happened?"

"They turned against their masters—attempted to escape. They took the tower as their own, barricaded the entrance, and defended it with the very materials they'd been using to construct it. The king's forces diverted irrigation canals to flood the base of the tower, destroying the foundation. The tower collapsed with the slaves inside. The king had each and every survivor killed for the insurrection. Before construction could resume, war broke out. Then famine. The old king died, a new one took his place, and Eurmeiminanki was forgotten."

Autumn considered his grim expression, the hollowness of his tone. "It must have been horrible," she said gently.

"Yes."

Despite her burning curiosity, she recognized his unwillingness to say any more about it. She tried to think of something else to say. Her gaze drifted over his body. "You know what? I think these—" she tapped one of the complicated sigils embedded in his skin "—look like writing."

He looked down at her finger, pressed to his bicep. He stared for a long time, until Autumn nervously withdrew her touch.

"Sorry," she said, realizing suddenly how pathetic every aspect of this situation was. She had somehow bullied a creature who existed solely for sex into suffering through some kind of platonic cuddle session because the few friends she did have were too busy for her and she hadn't enjoyed the peaceful company of a man in nearly two years. "I didn't think—"

He caught her hand and brought it back to his arm, pressing it there. "Nobody ever touches me—except to fuck me." He squeezed her hand. "It surprised me, to feel your touch without the urgency of arousal with it. But I enjoyed it. I am never touched in kindness, in gentleness, in curiosity. Don't stop, please." His cheeks were flushed purple, and he couldn't look her in the eyes.

Autumn melted against him, leaning her shoulder against his. She reached down until she found his hand and laced her fingers into his. It took him a second, but he finally reciprocated, curling his long fingers around her hand. He rumbled in his chest, a deeply contented sound.

Emboldened by his obvious enjoyment, Autumn pulled her hand from his and, urging Irdu forward, slid her body behind his, sitting with her legs spread around him. She dragged her fingernails lightly down his back.

Irdu shivered, pushing back into her touch. His tail was curled to one side, but the end flicked back and forth. Autumn continued to trace her fingernails over the broad, muscled expanse of his back, idly following tattooed lines and sigils. She pressed her thumbs into the line of muscle running up each side of his spine. She squeezed the tense muscles of his shoulders and the back of his neck. She slid her fingers up the back of his neck, threading through his thick, cobalt hair, to scratch at his scalp.

Irdu let out that rumbling groan again, head and shoulders slumping as if in defeat. He submitted to the gentle explorations of her fingers, groaning like an old dog whenever she found a sensitive spot. At any moment, she expected his leg to start kicking.

"*Autumn*," he moaned her name as she massaged around the base of his ears. The plaintive neediness in his voice sent a bolt of lust straight through her core. "*Autumn*," he gasped again, body going rigid beneath her touch.

He can feel when I'm aroused, she remembered, mortified. "I'm sorry," she said quickly. "Ignore me. I'm not touching you just so I can get laid. I want you to feel good. Just—"

Irdu twisted around, pinning her to the headboard, caging her with his powerful body. One clawed hand gripped her chin, forcing her to look into the inky black depths of his eyes.

"Never apologize for wanting me," he commanded, his voice a gravelly bass. "That, too, is a gift I never thought to receive."

"Oh," she breathed. The intensity of his gaze, the power of his body, the casual dominance of his touch—it all melded together into an explosion of pure *want*.

Irdu felt it as soon as she did, growling low in his throat. He dropped her chin and the two of them surged together. Autumn had one hand fisted in Irdu's hair, the other digging into the flexing muscles of his back as she wrapped her legs around his waist and sealed her mouth to his in a desperate kiss. She bit and sucked at his lips, flicked her tongue over the tips of his fangs, licked boldly into his mouth.

Irdu let the full weight of his body sink onto hers. Pelvis to pelvis, she felt the thick length of his cock, hard and heavy, pressed to the slick, hot seam between her thighs. He rolled his hips, grinding the length of his erection against her. Autumn gasped, arching her hips up, taking every bit of sensation she could. She panted as she clung to him, rocking against each languorous thrust of his hips. She was still wearing her night shirt and panties, and they suddenly felt like weighted nets, tangling her body, encumbering her freedom.

Irdu reared back, helping her peel the t-shirt over her head. He reached for her panties, and she lifted her hips as he slid them down the length of her legs. Then she was as naked as he was. They stared at each other, drinking in the sight of their shared arousal. Irdu's broad chest rose and fell with each rough breath. His skin was flushed purple along the crests of his cheekbones. His lips were swollen from her kisses. The dark scar across his throat looked livid against his flushed skin.

Autumn's gaze dropped to the furred expanse of his chest, golden piercings winking from each dark-blue nipple. She continued her perusal south, over the ridged muscles of his abdomen, following the tight V of his Adonis belt to the sculpted beauty of his erection—long and thick, flushed dusky purple, with a gleaming smooth crown, and a thickly veined shaft. To Autumn's surprise, he had more piercings than those she'd already noticed. Three thick golden barbells studded the underside of his cock. The first was positioned just below the head, the second an inch below that, and the third an inch below that.

"*Oh.*" She pushed herself up so that she could touch them. Irdu held stock still under her perusal. She trailed her fingers gently along the curving underside of his cock, stopping at each large barbell. She gripped the topmost one and tugged ever so gently. A spike of lust stabbed through her, and Irdu nearly doubled over on a groan.

"Does that hurt?" she asked, breath coming raggedly.

"Do it again," Irdu answered hoarsely.

She tugged a little harder this time, whimpering at the powerful surge of arousal.

Irdu fell forward onto his hands, head hanging as he shuddered through the overwhelming wave of her arousal. "Again!"

Autumn was wet and hot and throbbing with the need to have him inside of her, but the control she had over Irdu's pleasure was too good to rush. She caught one of his horns and used it to tilt his head back, making him look her in the eye as she gave the piercing a slow, sadistic pull. His brows drew together, his fathomless black eyes glazed with need as he panted through the exquisite torture. She knew he only enjoyed it because she enjoyed it—but that only made it hotter. The sight of such a powerful, masculine creature brought low by her sexual desire made her shiver and moan as another debilitating wave of pleasure rolled through her.

"*Autumn!*" Irdu rasped her name, somehow making it sound like both a plea and a command.

She felt an impending orgasm building inside like a thunder cloud. Just as with a storm, the air around them was thickly charged, redolent with the rising tension. Autumn was nearly mindless with the need to climb onto his cock and ride him to orgasm. But she wanted to draw it out more, torture them both, make the eventual release all the better.

"Poor Irdu," she purred in husky voice dripping with sex. "Are you hungry?"

"*Yes*," he panted, glazed, heavy-lidded eyes still held captive by hers. "*Please*," he begged.

She leaned back, pulling Irdu along by one horn. She drew her knees up, then parted them slowly, like the unfurling of a rose, revealing her glistening pink center.

He surged forward, hands sliding beneath her ass to hoist her up for his greedy mouth. He licked into her slit with one, long swipe of his tongue. Autumn arched her hips up with a choked whimper, quickly losing control of the situation. Irdu growled as he licked and sucked at her clit, his fangs pressing into her soft flesh. Pleasure coiled inside her, winding tighter and tighter, coming closer and closer to snapping free—

"Stop!" Autumn cried.

Irdu pulled his mouth away from her on a sloppy, sucking kiss. Hovering just above her swollen, glistening folds, he met her gaze and licked his lips. "Why?" he asked, his voice an inhuman growl.

"I want you inside me." She threw her arms open in invitation. Irdu wasted no time in accepting, climbing up her body until his hips were settled in the cradle of her thighs. She wrapped her legs around his waist, her arms around his neck, and took his mouth in a long, hot, needy kiss. She tasted herself on him, and as the pleasure of that lanced through her, Irdu's hips gave a wild buck, sliding his pierced cock over her exquisitely sensitive clit. She nearly came apart just on that one stroke.

"Inside me!" she ordered, pulling at him with her legs. "Now!"

"Yes," Irdu panted as he shifted to align their bodies. The broad head of his cock nudged against her slick folds, and then he was pressing into her.

"Oh!" He was big—painfully so—but somehow the pain only made her pleasure rocket higher as he steadily, mercilessly, fed every thick inch into her tight, wet channel. She bit at his shoulder and neck as he stretched her wide, until she felt she would split in half. "Irdu!" she whimpered. "Ah! Irdu!"

"Autumn, Autumn, *Autumn*," he rumbled back, nipping at her ear. He buried himself to the hilt and held there for a moment. They clung to each other, trembling and gasping for breath. Irdu filled her so completely, Autumn worried she wouldn't ever feel whole again, except when he was inside her.

"Perfect," she gasped, clinging to him until her fingernails dug into his skin and her heels drove into the thick muscles of his ass. His tail wove sinuously around one of her legs.

Shaking with the effort, Irdu began a slow withdrawal. Autumn mewled at the loss. His cock slid from her until only the head of him remained inside. And then, with a smooth, hard stroke, he plunged all the way back inside, seating himself with a slap of skin against skin. Autumn let out a little scream, toes curling, fingernails digging harder into his back. She felt his claws curl against her hips in answer.

"Go," she begged on a sob. "Again! Please!"

He drew back and thrust forward, steady and strong. Then again—a little faster, a little harder. Then again, and again, and again, until he was pounding into her with a frenzied need, driving both of them higher and higher to the thunder and lightning. Autumn was sweating, gasping, rolling her hips to meet each slamming thrust. She was so close—*so close*—

Irdu grabbed her face with one hand and brought his mouth down on hers in a kiss that was just as wild and brutal as the thrust of his cock. Instantly, Autumn came—flying apart into every individual atom that made up her being. She felt the atoms of Irdu coming apart with her, the essence of them both mingling together as they danced through the empty space between creation and destruction. Their heartbeats matched the endless spin of every galaxy, their breath the expansion of the universe.

At last, they reached the farthest edge of their pleasure, and slowly, inexorably, returned to corporeal reality. Hyper-aware of every point on her body, Autumn lay bonelessly beneath Irdu. She felt the press of the bed against her back, the wild disarray of her hair—a strand stuck to her sweaty cheek. She felt the sheen of sweat coating her entire body. She felt the pump of her blood, the gust of her breath, the flexion and contraction of every muscle. She felt the slide of her eyelids as she blinked, the rasp of her breath over her tongue and lips. But most of all— she felt Irdu. Big, hard, hot, and heavy. He was still inside her, all of his weight bearing down on her. His head was pressed to the mattress just above her left shoulder, one horn hooked in her afghan blanket.

She twisted to look at him, cupping his cheek. His lips were parted slackly as he panted for breath. His eyes were vacant and dazed, dancing with a whorl of vivid blue over endless black. Autumn watched the galaxy-like spin of color while she caught her breath, waiting for him to come back to her.

After a minute, the blue dispersed from his eyes. Slowly, the black began to recede until bright blue irises and elliptical pupils stared back at her. He blinked. Then blinked again.

"Are you okay?"

"Yes." She stroked her thumb along his cheekbone. His eyes slid closed as he leaned into her touch. "Are you?" she asked.

"Yes." Suddenly, he seemed to realize he was still on top of her, his claws still sunk into her hips. He released his grip and lifted himself off of her. "You should have told me I was hurting you!" he said, slowly easing his cock from inside of her.

She gave a little hum in her throat as the thick head of his cock passed through the tightest part of her entrance. "I'm fine," she told him with a soft smile. "I liked how it felt." She looked down at her hips to find new marks, some dotted with blood, added to yesterday's. She grinned at him and sat up. "Besides—I left my own marks on you." She traced her fingers along the gouged skin on his back. "Now you're mine."

Irdu stared at her, an unreadable mixture of emotions passing behind his eyes.

"Are you sure you're okay?" Autumn asked gently.

"Yes," he said, his voice a bit unsteady. He shifted and looped an arm around her stomach, pulling her back against his chest. He laid them both down and pulled the blankets over Autumn's cooling skin.

"Will you stay with me again?" she asked.

"As long as you will let me," he said, resting his chin on top of her head.

"Then stay as long as you can." Autumn turned off the long-forgotten TV and snuggled into him, feeling safe and content for the first time in years. Sleep was not far away, and she succumbed to it with a soft smile.

Chapter Four

The days passed slowly, the nights too quickly. As she'd requested, Irdu came to her at sundown. With time, they fell into easier and easier conversations with each other. She asked him about his human past, and his life as a demon. There were some things he was tight-lipped about. But as the nights passed, he opened up more and more to her.

Autumn made a point of giving Irdu platonic touches—leaning against him while they watched TV, dragging her fingernails gently over his scalp, giving him idle massages. Inevitably, those innocent touches turned sexual. After Irdu brought her to orgasm, he'd hold her until she fell asleep. She found herself staying awake later and later, talking with him.

Thanksgiving came and went, and Autumn had been invited to Liz's family's celebration. She had no doubt that it was a pity invitation. After breaking up with Dylan, Autumn had nobody to spend the holidays with. She had no extended family, her father was dead, and her mother lived in Florida. So Autumn accepted the invitation. Thanksgiving dinner at the

Cruz household was more of a late-lunch affair, and Autumn managed to slip out before sundown, returning to her apartment just before Irdu appeared.

She'd come to value her time with him so greatly that she was starting to worry herself. She couldn't seem to dampen her excitement for him. Even though all they really did was chat and watch TV, she had more fun with Irdu than she had with anybody else. As they got closer and closer to winter, the days grew shorter, and the nights longer, which meant even more time spent with him.

After a while, Autumn managed to bring him around on her love of hate-watching bad shows. To her delight, he offered blisteringly sarcastic criticisms that had her laughing so much her abs ached the next day. He'd confessed to a fascination with people—probably spurred by his inability to interact with them—so Autumn had started queueing up shows that featured large ensemble casts. One such show followed the rise of an antihero who started with nothing, but through grift and cunning, accumulated an empire of wealth and power. Irdu had been disgusted with the character and the show.

"Just another tower builder," he'd complained. It was the first time he'd asked her to stop playing a show.

The epithet replayed over and over in Autumn's mind. *Tower builder.* She began to understand that his disgust with "tower builders" permeated beyond entertainment. She saw it in the way his lip curled when she told him how wealthy her ex-boyfriend was, and that she'd walked away from their relationship with nothing but her clothes. She heard it in the frustrated noise he made when they watched a news segment about a law that criminalized homelessness. She felt it in the way his body tensed when she was leaning against him and explained how her workplace employed the owner's family members in all the highest-paying positions, even though they did little to no work.

His sensitivity to those things made her wonder more and more about his past, but she didn't want to pry too much. When she asked questions he didn't want to answer, he clammed up, and the evening turned stilted and awkward. But for the most part, things were easy and comfortable between them. Maybe too comfortable.

Irdu didn't just give her the best orgasms of her life and make her laugh until her sides hurt. He was also openly fascinated by her art. She had to remind herself over and over that their arrangement was temporary and would end any day, without any notice. She tried not to let herself get too attached. But when he stood in front of her in-progress painting, considering it with all the intensity of an art student in the Louvre, Autumn could feel her heart doing weird things inside her chest.

"This reminds me very much of the Russian Madonnas," Irdu said one evening.

Autumn nearly bounced off the floor in excitement. "That's exactly what I was going for!"

He was examining a portrait she'd nearly finished of her friend Liz, in which Liz held her baby Athena on one arm and a cup of coffee in the other hand. She had her cellphone pressed between her ear and her shoulder and a frayed afghan blanket was draped over her head and shoulders like a mantle. Like the Russian icons, there was a great deal of gold and filigree, but in Autumn's painting, the filigree formed a pattern of computer circuits, and instead of a halo behind Liz's head, there was an ominous golden clock face. Liz hated it, but she had said so in an admiring kind of way.

Irdu stared at it for a long time. "She's your friend?"

"Yeah, that's Liz. She and her husband Marcus are pretty

much my only friends." Embarrassed by the admission, she tried to tack on a dismissive laugh, but it was too late. Irdu looked over at her, sympathy in his eyes.

"Do I count as a friend?" he asked.

Her heart thumped. "Yes. Of course you do."

He turned back to the painting. "Do you do often paint portraits?"

"Sort of. I like to paint human figures, but the subjects are often conceptual."

Irdu tilted his head as he stared at the portrait of Liz. "You are very talented."

Her heart thumped again.

As the nights progressed, he took to examining her works-in-progress. He liked to watch her paint, and their evening routine shifted from watching television together, to Autumn painting while Irdu watched and asked questions.

She'd begun working in secret on a smaller portrait that she hid away in the closet at night. It took her several weekends during the daylight hours to complete it. She thought about waiting until Christmas day to give it to him, but then she rationalized that a demon whose existence predated the Old Testament probably didn't put a lot of stock in the holiday. Besides, Christmas was weeks away, and she didn't want to wait any longer to give it to him.

When he finally appeared, she practically threw it at him, she was so nervous for his reaction.

"I have a gift for you," she said, gesturing awkwardly to the painting, displayed on her easel.

It was done in an impressionistic style, because she hadn't been able to work off a reference photo or drawings. With bold, sketchy brushstrokes, she'd rendered a portrait of Irdu as a sensuous ingenue. He was seated on a throne made of twining rose vines. His vibrant blue eyes smoldered as he leaned forward, staring into the eyes of the viewer. The blue shades of his body contrasted beautifully against the dusky pink roses. What the portrait lacked in precision, it made up for in energy. Irdu's likeness radiated an alluring combination of emotional warmth and masculine potency.

Irdu stood in front of the painting and stared at it silently. His face was completely blank. After a long stretch of silence, Autumn began to get anxious. He hated it. He was angry. He was insulted. He was trying to figure out how to tell her—

"I can't believe this."

Autumn's heart stopped. "What?"

"Nobody has ever done something like this for me." He continued to stare at it. "When I was human, only the most elite had their likeness recorded. Kings. Gods." He shook his head. "I don't deserve this."

Her heart resumed beating. "Yes you do. It's my gift to you."

His grip tightened on the edges of the canvas. "I have no way of giving you anything in return."

"That's not how gifts work. Besides, you give me things I can never repay either."

Irdu regarded her skeptically.

"Comfort. Companionship. Happiness. Peace."

His skepticism faltered. "You don't think of me as..."

"As what?"

He sighed. "As a parasite?"

Her brows shot up. "Is that how you think of yourself?"

"Yes."

Autumn didn't know how to comfort him. "You're not a parasite," she said angrily. "You're kind and funny and wonderful. I look forward to seeing you all day."

Irdu's gaze lifted to hers. Something intense burned in his eyes, but neither of them was ready to acknowledge it. Whatever it was, it was too big, too terrifying. As if they could run away from it, they both surged into motion. Crashing together in a feral embrace, they tumbled wildly onto the bed where their bodies worked through the truths their minds weren't ready to consider.

Chapter Five

W eeks passed in that happy, but fraught stagnancy. The idea of changing anything between them was terrifying—changing could very well mean losing Irdu. But at the same time, Autumn was beginning to feel caged by the limitations of their relationship. She sensed it in Irdu, too.

Every night she fell asleep in his arms, and wished she could wake in them as well. In the mornings, she instinctively reached for Irdu. When she felt only an empty bed, she remembered that he was gone and some of her golden glow dimmed a little. But he'd be back at night, she told herself every morning.

Mid-December, she found herself staring down yet another Sunday full of daylight. She had nothing to do and nobody to do it with. She tried to distract herself by cleaning her apartment, but the distraction didn't last long. Within a few hours, she had the floor swept and vacuumed, the bathroom scrubbed, the kitchen wiped down, dishes put away, and the laundry done.

As she put clean sheets on her bed, she couldn't help but

think of Irdu. She checked the time, sighed, and looked out her window where the stupid sun was still high in the sky.

She knew Sunday was a more relaxed day for Liz and Marcus, so she texted Liz to see if she was free. Liz texted back almost immediately:

> Sorry, can't. I'm sitting in the airport right now. I'm flying out to D.C. this afternoon.

> What? Why?

> I'm spending a few days doing research in the National Archives for my book.

In addition to her regular journalistic endeavors with the Chicago Times Herald, Liz was writing a biography on Jane Addams.

> Ugh, fine. Have fun, you nerd.

> I'm the kettle, you're the pot.

> I'm not a nerd.

> You once told me that you have a favorite French court painter. That is a level of nerdery that I will never surpass.

> Jacques-Louis David managed to keep his head attached to his neck through three drastically different regimes. Can you imagine being such a good artist that Robespierre decides to spare you, even though you used to paint for Louis XVI?

> Point proven. You are a nerd.

They texted back and forth until Liz had to board her plane. And then Autumn was left alone with her thoughts—which mainly circled around Irdu.

Autumn didn't think she was the sort of woman who lost all sense of self in favor of a man. When she'd been with Dylan, his biggest complaint had been that she was argumentative and didn't care about any of his interests. On the flip side of the coin, they'd always gotten a certain amount of enjoyment from arguing with each other—things never turned nasty or personal. And as far as interests went, he'd never wanted to try hers either.

But with Irdu, she found herself unable to think of anything else. It was only to be expected, she reasoned. Irdu wasn't exactly an ordinary kind of guy. She wasn't turning into some man-obsessed drip. She was just—very reasonably—fascinated by her new supernatural sex buddy.

But that flippant description of Irdu felt somehow unkind. Disloyal, almost. *Lover*, she amended. *Fascinating, sweet, demon lover.*

Eventually, she gave in to the fact that she couldn't think about anything other than Irdu. So far, she'd resisted the urge to Google the things he'd told her about his human life. He was evasive about some topics, and so she tried to respect that he wasn't ready to share them with her. But with the whole of a lonely Sunday stretching out ahead of her, her will-power snapped. She opened her laptop and put her cursor in the search bar.

Tower of Babel, she typed. She had to try six different spellings of *Eurmeiminanki* before she finally got any hits. She fell down a rabbit hole of research—reading about everything from the Akkadian king Sargon, Mesopotamian cosmology, and Babylonian architecture, to early-Judaic monolatrism, the

Hebrew Bible, and the linguistic diversity of ancient Mesopotamia.

There were a surprising number of myths surrounding the destruction of a tower meant to reach the heavens, and a corresponding relationship to changes in language. She clicked between tabs, reading and re-reading them, considering the overlaps and divergences between them. None of the stories included anything about slaves rebelling.

Several sources connected the biblical Nimrod, architect of the Tower of Babel with Sargon of Akkad. And when Nebuchadnezzar was trying to rebuild the tower of Babel, he referred to a predecessor who'd built the original long before him—who could have potentially been Sargon. If Sargon was the king who'd constructed the original tower, then that would mean Irdu had been around since at least 2334 B.C. She clicked on a thumbnail image of an old Babylonian tablet describing Sargon's reign, and gasped out loud. The cuneiform writing looked exactly like Irdu's tattoos.

After scrolling through article after article about cuneiform, she returned her attention to Sargon—trying to find a connection to a possible slave rebellion. Trying to find anything about prisoners of war and slave labor, she clicked back to an academic paper about the ziggurat in Borsippa. If completed, it would have been the tallest structure in the entire Akkadian empire. It was likely originally constructed for the local god, Nabu—the patron deity of literacy and scribes.

Languages. Writing. Irdu's tattoos.

Autumn directed her research towards that—falling down another rabbit hole about cuneiform, its evolution over the rise and fall of various Mesopotamian kingdoms and empires. As a single writing system, it was used across multiple languages. Even when the old languages died and new ones took their place, cuneiform persisted.

A single writing system used to communicate across multiple languages... the collapse of a ziggurat dedicated to a god of writing... a slave rebellion... and Irdu's tattoos.

Autumn sensed a tenuous connection between those things. She poked and prodded and twisted and rearranged them in her mind, but try as she might, she couldn't bring them together into a clear answer.

Irdu clearly hadn't wanted to discuss it any further last night. Would he be annoyed if she brought it up again? Would he be willing to explain the meaning of his tattoos?

She checked the time on her phone and nearly jumped out of her chair with excitement. Her research had eaten up several hours. Her east-facing window was dark. Sunset was only half an hour away. Soon, not only would she get to see Irdu, but she'd have some answers.

Maybe.

While she waited for the sun to go the hell away, she read more about the symbiotic interplay between the Sumerian language and Akkadian. She was trying to figure out, based on her estimate of Irdu's age, whether he would've spoken Sumerian, or Akkadian, or both.

She was looking at Borsippa on a map of the ancient Akkadian Empire when she sensed a change in the air. She looked up and found Irdu standing in the center of her room, watching her with a cautious expression.

"Irdu!" She slammed her computer shut and launched herself at him. He caught her in his arms, his expression transforming to something both incredulous and joyful as she wrapped her arms around his neck and laid a happy kiss on his cheek.

"Hello," he said, sounding a little dazed. His embrace was almost painfully tight, and he gazed down at her with an expression of such earnest happiness that Autumn felt her heart expanding inside her chest.

"I missed you," she told him. "I missed you all day." She sounded like a child, but she couldn't hold back the tide of feeling.

"I missed you too," he told her. He leaned down and gave her another one of those sweet, heatless kisses. A gentle touch of undemanding affection. Autumn's heart swelled again. She pulled him towards the bed and propped up pillows so they could sit comfortably.

"What do you do when you're not with me?" she asked. "When you're in the Underworld?"

Irdu's expression shuttered and all the joy in him blinked out in an instant. "You don't want to hear about that."

"Sorry," Autumn said quickly, nearly choking on her regret. "I didn't want to upset you. I just want to know about you."

Irdu regarded her silently from that bleak, empty mask. "Know, then, that I live only when I am with you. When I am not with you... I am not myself. If others of my kind knew the joy you brought to me, they would find a way to destroy it."

"Why?'" Autumn asked, unable to stop herself.

The bleakness in his eyes was heartbreaking. "Because you are everything that is wonderful and good about the living world—things that are forbidden to my kind. When I am with you, I can steal a little bit of that for myself." He looked away from her. "For as long as I exist, my time with you, however fleeting, will be burned into my soul. And when you no longer need me, and I am summoned to another, I will comfort myself with the memories of the time I had with you."

Autumn's eyes burned with tears. "I don't want to let you go. I don't want anybody else to summon you from me."

He turned back to her, a sad smile pulling at his lips. He stroked his thumb gently beneath her eye, catching a tear before it streaked down her cheek. "I am yours as long as you want me."

Forever! Autumn stopped herself from blurting it out, staring at him in fraught silence instead. Someday, she would have to let him go. Whether it was because she'd resolved whatever need had summoned him, or because... she died. Someday she would have no choice but to leave him.

"You have to tell me about yourself," she said suddenly, urgently. "If we're going to be separated eventually, I need every piece of you that I can hold onto."

Irdu considered that for a moment. "I don't want to drive a wedge between us," he said. "My past is ugly."

"Just tell me this—were you human at Borsippa?"

Irdu met her gaze. "Yes."

"Were you—" her throat caught. "Were you one of the slaves?"

"Yes." He held her gaze, the blue of his irises intensifying. "I am the lowest of low, Autumn. I am a failed warrior, captured alive. I am a slave. I am a defeated rebel. And now I am a demon. A slave once again, and a parasite, whose very existence is dependent—"

She cupped his face with both hands, her gaze boring into his. "You're Irdu," she said, her voice wavering with emotion. "You are kind and generous. You take care of people who need it. You make me—them—feel safe and valued. Your history makes you *fascinating*, not pathetic. You have always fought your circumstances, no matter how desperate. That's admirable. That's... it's heroic."

Irdu stared back at her. Dark emotions shadowed his gaze. "I led the rebellion. I got them all killed."

"Would they have rather lived as slaves?"

Slowly, the bleakness eased from his eyes, and he looked back at her with a thoughtful expression. Satisfied, Autumn leaned against him, wrapping her arms around his torso and tucking her head beneath his chin. Irdu rumbled in his chest and relaxed against her. One strong arm encircled her, pulling her more tightly against him.

"I survived the ziggurat's collapse," he said, speaking above her head. She tightened her arms around him. "My legs were shattered, my ribs crushed. I was coughing blood with every breath. I would have died on my own within hours. But they captured me, made an example of me. I was sacrificed to the god whose tower I'd desecrated. They cut my throat and when I opened my eyes again, I was in the Underworld, and I looked like this." He held out one arm, blue and tattooed, tipped with curling black claws.

Autumn glanced at the thick scar across his throat, then took his hand and brought it to her mouth, pressing a kiss to his knuckles. "I'm so sorry that happened to you," she said fervently. "But I'm glad you came to me. I'm glad you have been in my life."

She felt a gentle touch on the top of her head—his lips. "I am grateful for every moment that brought me to this one, with you."

"*Irdu*." She buried her face in his chest. She'd never felt so strongly, so quickly, about somebody. It had taken months of knowing Dylan before she'd even been comfortable going on a tame movie date with him. Before Dylan, she'd only had two other relationships—a boyfriend in high school who'd been a platonic friend for three years before their brief senior-year romance, and a short-lived relationship just before she'd met Dylan, with a coworker she'd known for a year before he'd surprised her with a kiss.

"Now you must tell me something about yourself." Irdu said.

"Like what? I can hardly follow up 'Ancient Rebel Slave Who Died in the Name of Freedom.'"

Irdu chuckled, then sobered. "Tell me why a woman like you is lonely."

"A woman like me?"

"Kind. Funny. Beautiful."

Autumn blushed, which was a bit much, considering all the things they'd already done to each other. She looked down so that her hair hid her flushed cheeks. "I was with Dylan for a long time. I thought I would marry him. But he cheated on me. And... that was it, really."

"Are you still in love with him?" Irdu asked, sounding tense.

She laughed bitterly. "No. I came back early from a trip to visit my mother. He was in bed with her—in *our* bed. It was like everything I'd ever felt for him immediately turned to ash. All I felt was anger." She sighed. "But leaving him completely upended my life. I lost my job, my home, and my friends all in one fell swoop. Now I'm stuck in a shitty job, and this shitty apartment. I still have a couple good friends, but they're busy with their own lives..." She shrugged. "I've been alone ever since then."

"You don't have family?"

She shrugged again. Suddenly, she understood Irdu's reticence to talk about himself. It wasn't that she felt shame about her circumstances. It was just that they were so miserable, who would want to hear about them? "My dad died when I was thirteen. A car accident. My mom remarried when I was nineteen and moved to Florida with her new husband. I see her every couple years. Enough to keep up the pretense of a functional relationship."

Irdu looked askance at her.

"After Dad died, she kind of... detached from me. At first I think it was just normal grief. But when she started to get back to normal with everyone else, she didn't ever really come back to me. I think I reminded her too much of Dad. I'm the only physical remnant of his existence. Plus, I take after him—I've got his hair, his eyes, his nose."

"That's not an excuse for—"

"I know. I'm not saying it makes sense, or even that I forgive her—in fact, I don't. I don't think I'll ever stop being angry about it." Autumn had never said that out loud before, not even to Dylan. To her horror, she felt tears welling. "Shit," she breathed, wiping at her eyes.

Irdu looked down, made a distressed sound. Very gently so that his claws didn't touch her skin, he wiped tears from beneath her eyes.

"Sorry," she said, mortified. She tried to turn her face away, but he caught her chin and held her still so that he could swipe more tears from her cheeks.

"Don't apologize."

"You were enslaved and murdered, and you're not crying about it."

"It was a very long time ago. And I wasn't betrayed by my own mother."

That only made Autumn cry harder. Irdu pulled her into his arms, holding her tight. She clung to him, silent, as tears coasted down her face and soaked his chest. They stayed like that for long minutes. The tight clasp of Irdu's arms anchored Autumn, the warmth of his body and the steady rise and fall of his chest comforted her. Her tears began to dry up, leaving her face feeling puffy and tight.

"Anyways," she said on a shaky breath. "I eventually made a new family for myself. Dylan's parents took me in for the holidays—Christmas, Thanksgiving, Easter, all that. After we broke up, I obviously couldn't show up at his family events—even though I still can't help but think of them as my family.

His parents were—are—really sweet people." Autumn sighed. "And on top of that, we always threw a big Christmas party with our friends. After the breakup, everyone took Dylan's side. I was no longer on the Christmas guest list. Not last year, and not this year. So it'll be my second Christmas in a row spent by myself. I could go spend Christmas in Florida with my mom. Since she remarried, she's been warmer to me. But I still... I don't want to be around her when I already feel lonely."

Irdu squeezed her tightly, crushing the air from her lungs. "You deserve so much better than what you've been handed."

She looked up at him, tracing a gentle finger across the scar on his throat. "Not any more than you do," she said sadly.

He caught her hand, bringing it to his mouth for a brief kiss. "I can't regret anything that's brought me to this moment."

Autumn stared at him, wondering. Without the perfect storm of her mother's emotional abandonment, Dylan's betrayal, and the collapse of her social network, she never would've met Irdu. He'd been coming to her for less than a month—and she'd been cognizant of him for slightly less than that. And yet, if some other supernatural creature appeared in front of her, promising to wipe away all the sorrow of the last eighteen months in exchange for forgetting Irdu, Autumn knew, without a doubt, that she would decline the offer.

She didn't want Dylan back. She didn't want her mother back. She just wanted somebody she could trust, depend on, and love.

Love.

A pulse of alarm fluttered in her chest. She continued to stare at Irdu, struck dumb by awareness. The excitement she felt for him, the trust, the affection, the attraction... it was all headed in a very dangerous direction.

"Autumn?" Irdu touched her cheek, concern writ in the furrow of his cobalt brows.

"Sorry, I was just... thinking about something."

Irdu narrowed his eyes, clearly aware that she was evading. "What were you thinking about?"

Autumn hesitated. She didn't want to lie to him. And he had revealed so much of himself that he hadn't wanted to. "I... I think I'm... developing feelings for you." She looked away. "Serious ones."

Irdu stared at her, saying nothing.

Of course. Of course this was going to happen. The millennia-old sex demon who brought companionship to lonely women had to be used to his charity cases falling in love with him. Not directly, of course, but definitely with the dream lover who came to them every night in their time of need. And if Irdu hadn't yet fallen in love in return, that wasn't likely to change just because Autumn knew he was real.

"I don't know what to say," Irdu whispered.

"Don't say anything. I shouldn't have told you that." She shifted to put some space between them.

"No, please don't pull away. Listen." He tightened his grip, pinning her awkwardly against him. "I don't deserve..." his voice caught in his throat, becoming a deeper growl. "I have nothing to give you—any promise I make is meaningless... I— I'm—"

"It's okay," Autumn said, pushing against him, trying to get free. "You don't have to I shouldn't have said anything."

Irdu spun her around suddenly and pushed her onto her back, pinning her in place with the weight of his body. "*Listen,*" he said urgently. His eyes were inches from hers, burning with emotion. "If I had even the faintest hope of being with you, I would take it without question, damn whatever consequences there might be." He cupped her face with one hand. His fierceness faded, and his expression became bleak. "But I don't belong to myself. Someday, your hurts will heal, and I will be called away from you. And there's nothing I can do about it."

"I know," Autumn whispered hoarsely.

"I have never—*never*—enjoyed my nights on earth as much as I've enjoyed them with you. I've never been seen, known, or wanted before you. Your kindness, your humor, your openness are the sweetest joys I've experienced in millennia. Autumn, you are..." his voice caught, a growl reverberating in his chest. "You are precious to me. Don't ever think otherwise. It is the greatest shame of my existence that I can't truly offer myself to you."

The feeling of rejection fell away to something powerfully bittersweet—the joy of knowing that he felt the same way about her, combined with the agony of knowing that their days together were numbered.

"Then promise me something?" she asked, her throat tight.

"Anything in my power to do, I will do for you."

"No holding back anything. I want every piece of you I can have. And I will give you every piece of me. I'll tell you anything, give you anything, do anything. Just, let me have as much as you can give."

Irdu dropped his forehead to hers. "Yes."

Autumn swallowed away the sob that was squeezing her throat. She pushed away the sadness, tried to forget about the looming but unknowable end of their time together. He could disappear from her life at any moment, and she wouldn't know for sure until the sun rose the next day. But if she couldn't let that anxiety go, she wouldn't be able to enjoy what little time she did have with him.

Autumn tilted her head up, catching Irdu's mouth in a gentle kiss. A pleasured sound rumbled in his chest as he lowered his weight onto her. She wrapped her arms around his neck as the kiss deepened, lips parting, tongues twining. She needed to show him that he was more than sex, that the physical pleasure they shared was borne of an emotional connection she couldn't explain. And she sensed that Irdu was trying to tell her the same—she wasn't just survival, not just a means of living to the next night.

Autumn pushed Irdu up, disconcerting him at first. But when she peeled her sweater off and crawled into his lap, straddling and kissing him, he quickly set to work helping her. Working together, breaking apart only when necessary, they stripped Autumn's clothes away until she was as bare as Irdu. Hot skin pressed to hot skin.

The stark differences between them no longer seemed alien to Autumn. She loved every unusual feature that made Irdu so specifically himself. She loved the feel of his fangs and his claws digging into her skin, leaving marks behind. She loved the playful coil of his tail, wrapping around her legs, teasing her skin with gentle strokes of the tufted tip. His pale blue skin contrasted beautifully against the mellow hue of her own. His eyes—whether feline, demon black, or dancing with auroral blue—pierced her with an intensity unlike anybody else's. His horns...had delightful uses.

She laughed softly even as the memory sent a pulse of warm arousal straight to her belly. Irdu nipped her lip, trailed claws across one of her nipples, turning her laughter into a breathy sigh.

They held each other, moving slowly. Autumn traced her fingers up and down the flexing muscles of Irdu's back. Irdu cupped her jaw with one hand, his thumb and claw stroking over her fluttering pulse point. Tender, lingering kisses turned deeper, longer. Claw-tipped fingers traced along Autumn's body, making her shiver and flush. She threaded her fingers through Irdu's hair, scraping her fingernails over his scalp and down the back of his neck. He went still, claws pressed into her flanks, groaning as he leaned into the pressure of her fingertips.

He pulled back just enough to look her in the eyes. His had turned to unrelieved black, but the intensity of his gaze was unmistakable. A mixture of tenderness and ferocity reverberated between them as they held each other. And then Irdu leaned in, taking her mouth again in a long, deep, desirous kiss.

Autumn slid closer to him, until they were pelvis to pelvis, and locked her ankles together behind his back. His hips rocked, sliding the hard length of his cock through her slick folds, making her wetter, more sensitive. Autumn sighed her pleasure, squeezing her thighs around his hips and rocking back against him.

"Inside me," she whispered against his ear before biting it.

"Yes," he breathed. He slid his big hands beneath her ass and lifted her as easily as if she were a cat. He aligned the head of his cock with her entrance, teasing her as he nudged slowly inside.

"More, Irdu! Please!"

She writhed in his hold, and he relented, sinking her down on his cock with one powerful stroke, filling her completely.

"Oh!"

The sudden stretch was a pleasurable pain. Irdu held still, and Autumn clung to him, trembling. The immediate and total connection of their bodies crashed through her like a tidal wave. Unwrapping her legs from his waist, she shifted to kneel on either side of his thighs. Raising herself up on her knees, she slid slowly up the length of his cock, then sank back down. The electric sensation of his cock stretching her out, the feeling of his arms around her, of his big strong body trembling against hers, all overwhelmed her with physical pleasure—but also, an emotional closeness that seemed only to be able to find expression through physical connection.

Autumn wound her fingers through Irdu's hair again, and pulled his harsh, lovely face down to hers. "*Mine*," she growled against his lips.

"Yes," he panted, opening to her desperate kiss.

They held tightly to each other, Irdu's hands easing Autumn's weight as she rode him. They devoured each other, hungry kisses turning sloppy and desperate as the rhythm of their hips thrust faster and harder. Soon, they were simply pressed together, mouths open, breathing raggedly, as they rode closer and closer to climax.

"You're mine," Autumn told him again, her voice a desperate keen. "Forever. Mine."

"Always," he growled in return, breath hitching on a grunt as he bucked into her, harder and harder. "Yours, love, always yours."

He called me love, she thought. And then the precipice yawned open before them, and together they tumbled from the edge into oblivion. Blue exploded across her vision, a swirling, sparking miasma that enveloped her and carried her through the fall. *His eyes*, Autumn thought distantly, *I'm inside his eyes —inside him*. She felt him there with her, an embrace that enclosed her from every possible direction, the pressure both thrilling and safe, ecstatic and comforting.

Through the hazy glimmer of pleasure, Autumn sensed the void that surrounded them. It was an endless darkness that felt somehow cruel. The icy emptiness pressed in on them, a feeling like hundreds of cold, grasping hands. And in the darkness, gray, empty-eyed faces loomed. But their touch, their hollowness, could not penetrate the veil of electric blue light that surrounded them.

Slowly, the darkness faded, giving way to the mundane reality of Autumn's apartment. The flickering blue light swirled around them like a gentle tornado, disturbing nothing and imparting only warmth, and then it, too, faded away.

At last, there was only Autumn and Irdu, still tangled in a desperate embrace. Autumn released her grip on Irdu's hair, gently stroking the back of his neck while the blue haze danced and faded from his eyes. The black receded last, revealing indigo irises and narrow pupils. Irdu slumped against her with a shuddering sigh, his arms easing their crushing grip, his claws loosing from her skin. He pressed his face into the crook of her neck, his mouth moving softly over the tender skin there.

"It's never been like this," he said hoarsely against her neck. His claws traced a gentle trail up her spine. "You do something to me. Something different. Something...powerful." His tongue pressed to her skin, tasting the sheen of sweat.

"I feel it too," Autumn said faintly. The intensity of the pleasure he gave her was beyond anything she'd ever experienced before. But more than that, he seemed to... take her somewhere. She remembered the press of the darkness, the grasping hands, the vacant eyes in staring faces. She shivered.

"Are you okay?" Irdu pulled back so that he could see her face.

"More than okay." She pressed a kiss to his frowning mouth. She had a suspicion that she was seeing a glimpse of what awaited Irdu when the sun rose. But she didn't want to distress him, and she needed to think about it a little more. So she cupped his face and pressed one more kiss to his lips. "I'm starving," she said, easing off of his cock. "Do you eat food?"

Irdu watched as she slid off the bed and walked to the bathroom, the faint furrow between his eyebrows telling her that she hadn't convinced him of her alrightness. "No," he said. "I don't eat."

"Do you shower?" she asked, pausing at the bathroom door with a suggestive smile.

"I can start," Irdu said, surging from the bed and chasing her into the bathroom.

They showered together, kissing and clinging beneath the fall of water. They took turns soaping and massaging each other. Irdu gave her another orgasm, teasing her first by letting her ride his thigh as he kissed her, then driving her over the edge with his fingers. She came apart in his arms, slipping back into blue-veiled ecstasy. This time, she didn't feel the press of darkness around her. When she came back to herself, the black was fading from Irdu's eyes. She turned off the water and fetched a towel, rubbing Irdu down.

"What happens when I come more than once?" she asked him. "Do you get more energy?"

The languid pleasure left his face, replaced by hollow misery. "I promised I would hold nothing back, so I will tell you the truth, but I warn you it is unpleasant. Do you truly want to know?"

Autumn met his somber gaze, unflinching. "Yes."

Irdu took the towel from her and began drying her off. Autumn suspected it was so he didn't have to look her in the eye. "The energy I receive from you only goes partially to my own survival. The excess is siphoned away by the Host, to further her own ends in the Underworld."

"What are her ends, exactly?" Autumn asked.

"I don't know with any certainty, but I have a suspicion."

"And that is?"

"I believe she intends to break the barrier between living and dead, and expand her dominion into the living world."

Autumn shook her head. "I don't understand. How would that—"

"Everyone would die. Everyone." He wrapped the towel around her and nudged her out of the bathroom. "The Host believes that she could inhabit life and death simultaneously.

But she does not walk in the living world like demons do, and she does not understand it. Her takeover would destroy life itself."

"Is there anyone who can stop her?"

"There are those within the Underworld who are working against her. But it's dangerous. Her eyes and ears are everywhere. The slightest hint of mutiny is brutally crushed without regard to the innocence or guilt of those condemned. But the resistance exists. Just barely—but it is there."

Autumn turned to face him, her eyes wide, brows drawn together. "You're leading another rebellion, aren't you?"

His expression hardened for a moment. But as he gazed into her worried eyes, the hardness fell away to something like resignation. "Yes," he said simply.

Emotion welled in Autumn—fear, pride, worry, admiration, grief, and... and something deeper and more resonant. She wasn't sure what to do with that feeling. So she dropped the towel and threw herself at him, wrapping her arms around his broad torso, and pressing her face into the solid wall of his chest.

"Talk to me," Irdu urged, tilting her chin so that she looked him in the eye.

"I'm scared for you. And proud of you. And..." She twisted her chin out of his grasp so she could look away. When he reached for her again, she bit his finger.

"Ach!" He started in surprise. "Vicious little thing. Are you sure you're not a demoness?"

Autumn laughed, blinking away the burn of tears. Sobering, she looked up at Irdu, letting him see the storm of emotion playing across her face. "I don't want you to put yourself in danger. But I'm so... so... I'm just awed by your bravery. I can't believe you think of yourself as anything but a hero."

Irdu shook his head. "I'm only paying the debt I owe."

Autumn sighed. "You're so blind." She turned away from him and walked to her dresser to pull on a t-shirt and underwear. She padded over to her narrow kitchen. "You've worn me out, my lovely incubus. I need sustenance."

Autumn made herself a simple dinner of scrambled eggs while Irdu looked on. While she ate, they talked about easier topics. Irdu told her about his human life in the cradle of civilization. Autumn listened, rapt, as he described what he could remember of the family he'd once had. A loving mother, seven living siblings, and a father who'd died when Irdu was a boy.

"That wasn't so unusual back then," Irdu remarked. "Life was more... unreliable in those days. A simple scratch on the hand could kill a perfectly healthy man as surely as a slit throat." He rubbed absently at the scar across his own throat. "More slowly, though."

When she'd cleaned her plate, they returned to the propped-up pillows on her bed. They talked more. They kept on talking—about the things Irdu had seen and done, the places he'd been. Autumn told him about her relationship with Dylan, every excruciating detail from start to finish. Irdu rumbled his disgust with her ex, and she found herself feeling immeasurably lighter. For the first time in a long time, thinking of Dylan's betrayal didn't send her reeling back through all the bitter hurt.

They talked about Autumn's loneliness and the burden of Irdu's guilt. They talked about her empty Christmas and his need to atone for his failures. They talked long into the night, cuddled together on her bed, until Autumn's eyelids were drooping and her words were coming slow and clumsy.

"You need to sleep," Irdu said gently.

"I don't want to sleep. I only get to see you at night."

Irdu smiled. The look in his eyes made Autumn's heart

swell in her chest. "You have to work in the morning," he said in a failed attempt at sternness.

"Who cares about work?" Autumn said sulkily, even though—despite her antipathy towards her current job—she was typically an over-achiever.

"Go to sleep," Irdu whispered gently. Autumn felt her eyelids grow heavier.

"Is this—" she yawned luxuriantly ''—is this some kind of demon magic?"

Irdu chuckled. "No, love. You're exhausted. Go to sleep."

"Don't want to," she murmured, even as she snuggled down into her blankets. Irdu's chest was warm and solid against her back, his arm curled beneath her head.

"Go to sleep, and when you dream, I'll find you." He pressed a kiss to the top of her head.

Chapter Six

S he knew she was dreaming, because instead of her crappy, spider-infested apartment in late-December, Autumn was sitting at the end of the pier at her favorite Lake Michigan beach, under bright summer sunshine. The beach was filled with colorful umbrellas and towels. People played in the water while gulls swooped overhead and crowded hopefully near anybody who had food.

A shadow fell over Autumn and she looked up to see a tall man looking down at her. He was big and broad, with swarthy skin and blunt, unhandsome features. His raven-black hair fell to his shoulders. He looked familiar, but Autumn couldn't place him. The man eased down to sit beside her, dangling his legs over the edge of the pier.

"Do I know you?" she asked, bemused.

"I should hope so," he answered in a deep, growling voice that Autumn instantly recognized.

"Irdu? Why are you disguised again? I don't need the illusions."

"I think this is what I looked like when I was human." He

braced his arms on the lower rung of the railing and stared out across the lake. Blue water met blue sky, an endless vista with no horizon.

Autumn twisted to look at him, taking in the harsh lines of his features, the warm tan of his skin, the thick curl of his eyelashes. His eyes were a deep, chocolate brown, with round pupils. His black hair fluttered in the breeze, thick and a little messy. He'd dressed himself in a plain gray t-shirt, jeans, and sneakers. It was so strange seeing him like this. He was Irdu, but not. Somehow more familiar and more alien at the same time.

She reached out and traced his hairline where his horns should be and felt only smooth skin. She tucked his hair behind his ear, and found the tip of it curved instead of pointed. Seeing his features on a human face made her realize that some of what she'd taken for a demon's naturally harsh appearance was actually a broken nose that had healed without being properly reset.

"Smile," she said.

He turned his head towards her and humored her with a toothy grin. Flat, human teeth.

His smile faded. "You don't look happy to see me."

"I don't know why, but it makes me sad to see you like this."

His eyebrows—black—shot up. "You prefer my demon form?"

"It's not that, exactly." She thought for a moment, turning her gaze back out to the endless blue in front of them. "Seeing you as a human—yourself, but human—reminds me of everything terrible that's happened to you. Everything that's been taken from you. But it's also a reminder that, if you'd gotten the life you deserved, I would never have met you. I wouldn't know you if you were human."

His features flickered and faded until the demon Irdu sat next to her on the pier. She reached out and cupped his face, brushing her thumb across the tip of one fang. The benefit of a dream meant that nobody ran shrieking and screaming from the sight of him. In fact, nobody reacted at all.

"How were you able to create this?" She gestured to the beach. "Can you see my memories?"

"No. This was your dream. I just walked into it." Sunlight gleamed over his features, making him look even less human than he did in the low light of her apartment.

"You can be in the daylight in dreams."

"Yes." He tilted his head back and closed his eyes, letting the sunshine soak into his skin. Autumn smiled, and suddenly felt bad for asking him to drop the human illusion. So many things had been taken away from him. In her dreams, he could have them back, if only for a little while.

Looking back at the beach, she swung her dangling feet. "I used to come to this beach when I was a kid—when both of my parents were alive. We'd come here almost every weekend in the summer. Do you want to see more of the beach?"

Irdu got to his feet—clawed, elongated paws rather than feet—and held out a hand to her. She let him pull her up, and hand in hand, they walked down the pier and the beach.

"If you could be human again, would you?"

"If I could be human with you."

Autumn's throat tightened. If only. Swallowing past the welling emotion, she steeled herself to ask a question that had plagued her since she'd first realized what Irdu was. "We promised to tell each other everything."

Irdu's hand tightened on hers. "Yes."

"Is there a way to release you from your current circumstances? A way in which you can live and be free?"

Irdu was silent.

"Please. Just tell me."

"Yes. There's a way."

"Then why don't we try—"

"*Because it would require me to trick a mortal into taking my place in the Underworld.*"

Autumn's hopes fell and shattered. "Oh."

"*I would* never *do that.*"

"*I know you wouldn't.*"

"*I wish I could tell you that I'd do* anything *to stay with you, but I can't—*"

"*I would never expect you to. I would never ask that of you. I know you wouldn't be able to live with the guilt.*" *Autumn thought for a moment. "I probably wouldn't be able to either."*

The corner of Irdu's mouth lifted at her reluctant admission. "I know you wouldn't be able to. You're too good for this world or the next."

With a start, Autumn realized she might eventually be joining Irdu in the Underworld. "Does everybody who dies go to the Underworld?"

Irdu slid a worried glance at her. "Why are you asking this?"

"*I'm not going to kill myself," Autumn said, appalled.*

He looked forward again. "Yes. All souls journey to the Underworld."

Autumn was quiet, thinking.

"*Your silence is unnerving, considering the topic," Irdu said.*

"*I'm not going to kill myself!" She insisted again. She couldn't help laughing at the morbidity of their conversation. "Let's get in the water."*

They rolled up their pants and waded into the lake, falling into a conversation about Autumn's childhood memories of visits to the beach.

"*My dad would put his hands together, and I'd step on them, and he'd just* launch *me. So high, and so far!"*

Irdu grinned at her and laced his fingers together, forming a step with his hands. "Want to try?"

"My clothes will get wet!" At his expression, she remembered. "Oh. Right. This is a dream. Okay then, let's see what you've got."

Laughing and playing with Irdu, her dream eventually eased back into the oblivion of sleep.

AUTUMN WOKE TO THE ANNOYINGLY CHEERFUL TONE of her weekday alarm. She reached for her phone, but froze as she felt the heavy warm weight of an arm curled around her waist. It took her only a split second to remember—

"Irdu!" She silenced her phone and twisted to him, pressing a happy kisses all over his face. "You're still here!"

He smiled under her onslaught. "I have only a few minutes before the sun rises."

Autumn cast her eyes to the window. The sky was lightening to gray at the edge of the horizon, faint light gleaming over rooftops. She curled back into Irdu, holding him tight.

"The sun sets before I get home from work. Will you be here when I get back?"

"Of course."

Autumn snuggled tighter against him. "I don't want you to leave."

He clutched her tightly. "I don't want to leave."

But he had to. Autumn's arms suddenly collapsed around empty air. She reached out uselessly, hand closing on nothing. The bed was still warm where he'd lain, but Irdu was gone. She sat up, looking around her quiet, empty apartment.

⁓

"OH, WOW. THAT'S A GOOD LOOK FOR YOU," THERESE said snidely when Autumn walked into work.

Autumn looked at her outfit. She was in the process of

taking off her double-breasted wool coat, revealing a blue button-down shirt, covered in a repeating pattern of tiny chickadees. It was one of her favorite shirts. "What are you talking about?"

Therese gave Autumn one of her patronizing smiles and tapped her back.

Autumn looked over her shoulder and found a pair of her underwear stuck to her coat. They were the pair Irdu had peeled off of her and flung across her apartment last night. A goofy grin stretched her lips. She turned away from Therese to hide the happy flush that suffused her cheeks.

"Uh, whoops." She shoved the underwear into her bag. "Laundry gets so staticky in the winter."

"Right," Therese said skeptically.

Autumn nearly choked on the laughter she was trying to suppress. She floated through the rest of the day on a cloud. When Colton somehow managed to convert the recently finished pamphlet files to the wrong color mode and then emailed them to the wrong printer with an order for five thousand, Autumn just laughed and got on the phone to fix it. When Kyle draped himself over the top of her cubicle wall and told her effusively how *beautiful she looks in that shirt*, Autumn smiled maniacally and told him she found it in a dumpster.

"There was some kind of weird-smelling slime on it, but it still had all the tags on! And the slime washed right out."

"Oh. Uh. Good find."

Autumn grinned as Kyle backed away.

Despite her buoyant mood, Autumn was excruciatingly aware of each individual grain of sand filtering through the hourglass of her workday. She glanced at the time every two minutes—continually astonished to find that only two minutes had passed. She took lunch early and left the office to call Liz. Expecting to leave a voicemail while Liz was occupied in the

National Archives, she was surprised to hear her pick up the call.

"Hey, sorry to bother you. I was wondering if you know any experts on ancient Mesopotamian languages and cuneiform." Liz wrote for the Arts and Culture section of the *Chicago Times Herald*. She had contacts across an unbelievable number of fields.

"Yeah, actually. Leila Kader. She's an associate professor of history at the University of Chicago. She wrote her dissertation on the divergences between the various accounts of Inanna's descent into the Underworld."

Autumn's breath caught. A myth about a journey into the Underworld—contemporary to the time when Irdu died and became a demon? "Is that a story about a living human going into the world of the dead?" she asked.

"No, she was a goddess. Leila can tell you all about it. I'll text you her info. She loves talking about this stuff. Why do you need to know about Mesopotamian mythology?"

"A personal project," Autumn hedged, letting Liz believe she meant one of her paintings. "Well, I better let you go," she said before Liz's journalist senses detected that Autumn was hiding something.

"Alright. Talk to you later."

With the remainder of her lunch break, Autumn texted Leila Kader.

Hi, Dr. Kader, This is Autumn Havener. Liz Cruz gave me your phone number. I'm looking for somebody who can answer some questions for me about ancient Mesopotamian mythology and cuneiform. If you've got the time, I'd love to buy you a coffee and pick your brain.

The historian responded almost immediately.

> Definitely! When did you have in mind?

Not after work, Autumn quickly decided. That would cut into her Irdu time.

> Could you meet sometime tomorrow? Any time or place that's convenient for you, during the day.

> Absolutely!

She gave Autumn the name of a coffeeshop near campus and told her to be there at noon.

> Thanks so much. See you tomorrow!

"DECIDED TO KEEP YOUR PANTIES *UNDER* YOUR clothes?" Therese sniped when Autumn returned to the office.

Autumn laughed as if they were just two friends bantering. Therese gave her a baffled look. Autumn had never figured out why Therese hated her, but she was too happy to care. In a few hours, she'd go home to Irdu. Therese could be as caustic and abrasive as she liked.

Thanks to another one of Colton's mistakes, Autumn left work forty-five minutes late. The sky was dark. The sun had set more than half an hour ago. Irdu might already be in her apartment, waiting for her. She hurried to the train, desperate to get home.

When she got to her place, the sun had been down for an hour. She missed the lock with her key twice before she finally wrenched the door open and burst inside. She looked around. Unless he was hiding in the bathroom, there was no Irdu.

Her heart dropped into her stomach. Was it over already? The last few days had been the happiest she'd had in a long time. Maybe that was all it took. He'd given her a brief reprieve from loneliness and moved on to the next woman.

Numbness washed over her. Still wearing her coat and boots, with her bag still hung on her shoulder, she went to her bed and dropped face first onto it. She lay there for a long time, listening to the sounds of traffic below her window.

"Bad day?"

Autumn sprang off her bed and spun around. Relief and joy crashed into her. "Irdu?"

"Hello, Autumn." He stood in the center of her tiny apartment, looking pleased. She launched herself into his open arms, burying her face against his chest and holding him as tightly as she could. "Is everything alright?"

"Yes. Now it is. Where were you? The sun set an hour ago."

"I didn't want to enter your home when you're not there."

"You're welcome here any time." She pulled back to look up at his face. "When I got home and you weren't here, I thought you were gone for good."

Irdu adjusted his embrace, picking her up and carrying her to the bed. "I'm still here. As long as I can be." He set her down on the bed and began removing her shoes.

She sighed and slipped out of her coat. "You can come here as soon as the sun sets. I don't mind. I like knowing you'll be here when I come home."

He nodded, setting her boots on the floor.

"I mean—you don't have to," she said quickly, realizing how demanding she sounded. "If there's something else you want to do."

Irdu nodded again. His hands went to the waist of her trousers.

"What are you—"

He pulled the zipper down.

"Oh! Wait, listen. I need to tell you—"

He tugged her pants down her hips.

Autumn giggled, but caught his wrists, trying to hold him still. "It's important for you to know that I don't want you to be my slave. I know you're not exactly free to live as you please, but I don't want you to ever do something you don't—"

Irdu tugged out of her grasp. His pupils ate up his eyes until they were entirely black. She stared at the change, arrested for a moment. His eyes usually only seemed to change when she felt her own arousal spike. And while she was certainly warming up, she was mostly just having fun wrestling with him.

He took advantage of her momentary stillness to keep undressing her. His fangs glinted against his skin as he grinned, peeling her pants the rest of the way down her legs. She kicked them away, but wrestled with him when he reached for the buttons on her shirt.

"I'm trying to be serious!" She twisted in his arms, catching one clawed hand as it snaked towards her buttons.

"I'm taking you very seriously." His other hand snuck around, popped her top button open.

"Hey!" It was taking effort not to giggle and rip her shirt off for him. She twisted like an eel, evading his sneaky hands. He caught her hips and turned her around, throwing her onto her back and pinning her in place by straddling her. He opened the next button.

Smiling devilishly, Autumn buttoned her top one back up. Irdu opened a third button, she closed the second one.

"Witch!" he growled with a crooked, fanged smile.

She giggled and refastened another button. Irdu caught her wrists and pinned them over her head with one hand. With his other hand, he quickly unbuttoned her shirt. His claws were surprisingly deft. He flipped her shirt open, revealing her naked breasts. Her nipples tightened in the open air. Irdu dipped his head, sucking one, then the other. With her hips pinned by his bodyweight and her arms held above her head, she was helpless to do anything but receive the pleasure he wanted to give her.

"Irdu—ah! *Irdu.*" She gasped for breath. "I'm trying to—oh!—tell you that I don't want you—*oh!*—to feel like I'm—"

Irdu brought his mouth to hers, silencing her with a hard kiss. "There is nothing you could ask me that I would not want to do for you." He kissed her again, deeper, longer, until she was writhing underneath him. "If I were free, I'd still want to be your slave."

"No, don't say that. You're—" Her objection was swallowed up by another kiss.

"I'm *yours,*" he growled. He cupped one of her breasts, pinching her nipple. "Say it." It was somehow both a command and a plea.

"Mine," Autumn gasped, arching into his touch. Heat and moisture bloomed between her thighs. "You're *mine.*"

"Always." He shifted, stretching his legs out and insinuating his hips between her thighs. She spread her legs for him, welcoming the hot pressure. "And if you want me here at sundown, I'll be here. Happily. Because I'm yours."

She panted as he slid his erection over her slick folds.

"When you want a hard cock to ride, I'm your slave. If you want a face to sit on, you use mine." He punctuated each statement with a thrust, bearing down on her sex with delicious friction. "And if you just want to be held, to talk, you use me. Anything I can give you—sex, comfort, safety—you take from me. Why?"

"Because you're mine!" Autumn nearly sobbed the words as he set a delicious rhythm, gliding over her swollen, glistening folds, but not inside her.

"Yes. Yours, love. Now, tell your slave what he can do for you."

"Please, inside me," she begged. "I need you inside —*ohhhh.*"

He filled her slowly, his thickness stretching her just to the pleasurable side of pain. Autumn could see the moment when their shared pleasure staggered him—the determined set of his jaw giving way to a slack mouth and a low moan. With his cock wedged deeply inside her, his obsidian gaze met hers and something heavy seemed to pass between the two of them. Her heart lurched inside her chest.

Irdu lowered himself to his elbows, cupping her face as his hips rocked a slow, potent rhythm against hers. She rolled to meet him on each thrust, her parted lips pressed to his cheek, her labored breaths gusting over the side of his face. The intensity of their connection, the rawness of the physical sensations, overwhelmed Autumn, driving her quickly to the edge of climax. She clung to him, perched on that precipitous edge, but not yet tipping over.

"Take what you need, love," he panted against her ear. "Let me give it to you."

"I want to give you something," she breathed back. "Want to make you—"

"Give me your pleasure," he growled, thrusting deeper, harder.

"*Yes.*"

"You take what I'm giving you—" he gritted out "—and give it back to me. Take me with you, love." He let out a gasping breath. "Take me with you—"

"Yes!" Autumn dropped into the acute pleasure that only Irdu could give her. She was distantly aware of her body, trembling and arching, caged beneath Irdu's mass. But her mind was a riot of some other kind of awareness.

Sparkling blue aether swirled around her, a tender whirl-wind that lifted her and carried her away through a void of eternal darkness."

Again, she felt the press of other entities, other souls. They gathered around the edges of the protective aether, grim, empty, watchful. Autumn was surrounded by the warm, exquisite embrace of the swirling blue quintessence, but the edge of her mind was aware of the desperate emptiness gnawing at the edges of her safety—a hunger that burned like dry ice. She shivered and twisted within the dancing light, letting it carry her safely through the darkness.

She returned to herself in gradual increments, the darkness fading from her mind's eye until she became aware of a burning pain in the muscle that sloped between her neck and shoulder. The glowing blue incandescence surrounded them both, and Irdu's face was buried against her neck, his lips pressed to her skin, his teeth sinking into her. He was frozen above her, still trapped in the ecstasy of their climax.

After a moment, she felt his tongue move against her skin, and he released her from his bite with a gasp. "Autumn!" He lifted his head. His eyes danced with shifting veils of blue—like a faraway view of the same light that had enveloped them in her own mind.

The dancing light faded from his eyes. The black receded slowly. He blinked, and his gaze found hers. His face was stark with abject horror. "I'm sorry!" Still breathing roughly, he lifted his weight from her body and pulled out of her. "Are you alright?"

Autumn traced a finger over the place he'd bitten, feeling the two puncture wounds his fangs had left. She grinned at him. "I'm good. I liked it."

"You—*what?* I bit you! I've never lost control like that! I can't believe I—"

"*Shhh.*" She leaned up, looping an arm around his shoulders, and brought her mouth to his neck. She bit down—and not lightly. Irdu grunted, the muscles of his back tensing beneath her arm. "There," she said, releasing him. "Now we're even."

"You don't understand. I've *never* done something like this. What you give me—" he shook his head in disbelief. "I've never experienced the like."

"Good," Autumn told him fiercely.

"How can you—"

"I'll bite you again if it'll convince you I like it."

He slumped to the side, stroking one clawed hand down the center of her sweating body. "I can't believe you," he said, in a tone of wonder that wrapped around her like a warm hug.

"Same," Autumn assured him, curling against him. "It's kind of strange though. Lately, there's—" Autumn stopped herself from telling him about the darkness, and the presences she sensed there. If she gave him any reason to fear for her, she worried he'd do something drastic in an effort to protect her. Like stop coming to her.

Irdu pushed himself up on one elbow, frowning down at her. "What? Tell me."

"It feels like I leave my body, when I come," she said, telling him a portion of the truth. "I've never felt that before."

Irdu was quiet for a moment, searching her face. "Does it frighten you?"

"No. It feels amazing." Except for the bit where a bunch of hollow-eyed voyeurs stared hungrily at her.

Irdu's frown deepened. "What are you not telling me?"

Autumn pushed herself up and kissed him. "Don't look at me all suspicious-like. Can I draw you?"

Irdu recoiled, completely thrown by the change in topic. "*Draw me?*"

"Yes. I've already painted you, but I had to do that by memory. I'd like to capture a more accurate likeness."

"Why would you want to draw me?"

"Because I haven't drawn a live model in forever. And you are possibly the most interesting live model I will ever see in my life."

Irdu considered it, looking as if he'd very much like to say no.

"I thought my willing slave would do anything for me?"

He sighed, slanting her a wry look. "Fine."

Autumn grinned and bounced off the bed to fetch her sketchbook. She peeled her sleeves down her arms, flinging away the button-up shirt and pulled on an oversized t-shirt and underwear.

"What am I supposed to do?" Irdu asked.

"Stay just like that." Laying on his side, braced on one elbow, his tail curled languidly over his hip.

Autumn settled into the chair beside her dresser, sizing him up as she sharpened her drawing pencil. Irdu stared back, a mixture of amusement and uncertainty. She knew he didn't see his demon form as anything that could possibly be attractive. Even after she'd told him she didn't like the illusions, he appeared to her in human form in her dream. The human he used to be. Autumn understood suddenly that his physical form was a constant reminder of everything he'd lost—that he saw it as a barrier between them.

She began shaping the base of his figure, loose lines that captured the silhouette of him, the boldest shadows and highlights.

"It's nice to make actual art," Autumn told him as she drew.

"You don't enjoy your work," Irdu said after several minutes of silence. "That is, I mean your employment."

"I do and I don't. At best, it has no artistic or spiritual value. At worst, it actively degrades the importance of real art."

"But?"

"But I'm good at it, and I like being good at things." She fell silent for a moment as she etched in the rough beginnings of his features. "And I'm currently working at a nonprofit. So, my designs are technically soliciting money for a good cause instead of enriching some corporation—even if the organization is useless."

"Useless?"

Autumn explained her theory that the Weldon Foundation was purely a front for the filthy rich founder to illegally shift money—and that very little actually went to the causes the Foundation supposedly supported.

"Some things never change," Irdu said wearily.

"Human corruption?" Autumn asked.

"That, yes." After a moment he said, "But I've witnessed great acts of kindness, of sacrifice, as well."

"Yeah?" Autumn asked hopefully.

"Yes." He began recounting the time he'd seen all the elders of a village form a human barrier between their people and advancing pillagers. The pillagers were a horse people, with better weapons and superior numbers. The village's warriors had had no hope of defending the village. To everyone's utter shock, the pillagers admired the elders' courage, and spared the village.

"Really?"

Irdu nodded. "They expected to die—to give just enough time for the young and healthy to escape the oncoming raiders."

Autumn's throat tightened. "That's both ugly and beautiful."

"Humanity," Irdu said thoughtfully.

A comfortable silence descended again. Autumn moved to

the foot of the bed, so she could see the details of Irdu's body up close. As she sketched the faint tattoos wrapping around his biceps, it suddenly occurred to her that now was the perfect opportunity to copy down the cuneiform ideograms for her meeting tomorrow with Leila Kader. She flipped to a fresh page in her sketch book and began copying as many individual characters as she could identify.

"What are you doing now?"

"Drawing your tattoos." She refrained from telling him about her meeting with Leila Kader. She suspected he wouldn't like it. And she knew he wouldn't stop her, or even ask her not to do it, but his unhappiness would make her feel guilty.

She felt guilty anyway, as Irdu lay trustingly on her bed, watching her through heavy-lidded eyes.

"What will you do tomorrow?" Irdu asked.

Autumn looked at him, startled. "Why?"

"I'm curious what you do when I'm not around."

"Oh. Well. Work, mostly." She looked back down at her sketchpad. "I'm... I'm meeting someone for lunch. And I have to mail out my mom's Christmas gift."

"You give her a gift?"

Autumn shrugged. "She always sends me one." She made a face. "And it's probably the only one I'll be getting this year."

Irdu said nothing, watching her with a speculative look on his face.

"You know," Autumn said, refining the points on a particularly complicated ideogram, "It seemed like *you* were the one who started things today."

"By 'things' you mean sex, I assume."

"Yes."

"Hmm."

Autumn lifted her gaze from her sketchpad. "Well?"

"I've been thinking about that myself," he said, expression turning thoughtful.

"Your eyes changed pretty early into it, and you said your eyes change in reaction to *my* arousal."

"Yes."

"But if you started undressing me before I was even—"

"Are you upset?" He asked, sitting up abruptly.

"No! I liked that you wanted something from me without being driven by my needs." She closed her sketchbook and set it aside. Crawling to Irdu, she wrapped her arms around his neck and slid into his lap. "Is it possible that you can feel sexual desire, independent of mine?"

Irdu looked somber. "Does it bother you that I can't?"

Autumn opened her mouth to tell him no, but remembered their vow to give each other everything—including the truth. "A little," she admitted. "It feels one-sided—like the things you do for me are only for my benefit. I wish I could give you pleasure without worrying about what gets me off. I wish I could make you come without losing my own control. If I could, I would tease you until you begged for release."

Irdu grinned. "It's not all one-sided. I can't feel pleasure without you—but what you give me is beyond anything I've ever experienced before."

"Are you sure you can't? It really seemed like—"

"I wish it were my own. I certainly felt some sort of... excitement. But I think it was anticipation for the pleasure I knew we would share—not anything innate within myself."

"Oh." Autumn tried not to sound too disappointed and failed.

"You already have me on my knees. I'm positive that I've begged you more than once."

Autumn smiled at that. "Yes, you might have..."

"I can try harder." He leaned in his lips hovering just a hair's breadth above hers. "*Please* let me taste you."

Smiling wickedly, Autumn leaned back. "No."

Irdu followed her, closing the distance between them without touching her. "*Please*," he purred, lips stretching into a wicked, fang-baring smile.

Autumn let out a shuddering breath, and Irdu's gaze went black. "I can't tease you when I want you more than you want me," she complained wryly.

Irdu sat back from her, his smile falling away. The black faded from his eyes. "Is that what bothers you?"

"No, I—"

Irdu surged forward, catching her face between his hands. He looked hard into her eyes. "You promised you'd give me everything. Don't lie to me."

Eyes downcast, Autumn sighed. "Yes. *I* want you. But you only want what I want because you have no choice."

Irdu's hands gentled on her face. He stroked his thumbs gently along her cheekbones. "I wish I could let you inside my mind. You'd understand that your fears are completely unfounded. I have never cared for someone as much as I do you. I've never felt the way you make me feel. I've never looked forward to sex the way I do with you. Never. My way of wanting may be different from yours, but it's real. And it's only for you."

That sounds like you feel your own sexual desire, Autumn thought impatiently, but she wasn't going to push him to say it. He clearly didn't believe it was possible, and who was she to contradict the person who'd been doing this for millennia?

Placated either way, Autumn tipped her chin up and gave him a gentle kiss. "Because you're mine," she told him.

His eyes turned black. *I'm not there, yet*, Autumn thought

with a spur of hope. *This is yours.* Even so, the sight of him surrendering to need stoked an answering arousal in Autumn. She was too hopeful, too happy, to tease. She pressed her lips to his, sliding her hand down to find his erect length and guide him into her. They rocked together, clinging, kissing. Climax came in drawn out, languid waves. Autumn saw the bright blue veil wrap around them, and beyond it, the darkness filled with hollow faces.

Irdu recovered more quickly, his eyes already receding back to their normal blue irises and elliptical pupils when Autumn opened her eyes. She brushed her fingertips along his brow, taking in the earnest affection in his gaze, the relaxed set of his harsh features.

"It's getting late," Irdu told her softly.

She reached for her phone to check the time. It was two hours later than she would normally go to sleep, which meant she'd get less than six hours of sleep. Even so, she changed her morning alarm to go off earlier. "Will you come to me when I dream?" she asked.

"Of course."

She clicked her lamp out and lay in Irdu's arms, waiting for sleep to wash over her. The contentment she felt in his arms went so far above and beyond what she thought she'd had with Dylan that it was almost laughable now. Had she really thought to marry him some day?

On the heels of that thought, a darker one came to her— *you'll never marry Irdu.* No matter how happy they were together, someday, maybe soon, they would be parted from each other. She let out a pained breath.

"Are you alright?" Irdu's deep voice rumbled next to her ear.

You promised you'd give me everything. Don't lie to me. "No. I'm worried about losing you."

His arms tightened around her, but he was silent. There was nothing he could say.

Chapter Seven

"**H**ello, love." *Irdu wore his human face again— swarthy skin, broken nose, warm brown eyes. His black hair curled messily, blowing around his face in a teasing wind. She didn't bother telling him to get rid of the illusion. He wanted to be human for a little while, and she was grateful that she was the person he could do that with.*

They sat at the top of a mud-brick ziggurat, overlooking the bustling streets of an ancient city. The city was encircled by a tall wall. From their vantage point above the ziggurat, Autumn could see the green farm fields outside the city walls, cut through with snaking irrigation canals. Down in the city streets, people and animals streamed past covered market stalls.

"Is this where..."

"Borsippa," Irdu confirmed.

Autumn inhaled sharply. "Why would you want to bring me here?"

"You often ask about what the world was like when I was human. It's easier to show than tell. What do you think?"

"It's fascinating. But macabre, considering what happened to

you here." Autumn turned her gaze back to city. "Can we walk in the streets?"

Irdu took her hand, and suddenly they stood on the edges of a packed-earth street in the shadow of a towering wall. A man and woman passed by them, dressed in brightly colored robes, elaborately draped, belted at the waist, and decorated with tassels and fringe. Their dark hair was fashioned into curls, ornate metal jewelry encircled their throats, fingers, wrists. Up ahead, less finely dressed people made up the bulk of the crowd, wearing shorter, belted robes and little jewelry. Laborers—men—dressed only in wrapped loincloths stood atop the wall, heaving bricks into place.

"It's not perfect," he told her. "My memory is a little hazy."

"Well, it's been several thousand years," Autumn allowed.

Irdu took her hand and pulled her towards the stretched awnings of a street market. Goats, chickens, and stray dogs milled among the people. They passed another temple, a square building, towering high above the street, but nowhere near as tall as the ziggurat they'd just left. Bas-relief sculptures decorated the walls leading up to the temple.

"What's that?"

"The temple of Inanna."

Autumn stiffened beside him. Inanna—*the very figure whose descent into the Underworld may provide the clues Autumn needed to... what? Save Irdu? Was it even possible? She glanced sidelong at him.*

Irdu's gaze traveled over the city street, his expression remote.

"Does it bother you to remember this?" Autumn asked.

"I tried to wait for you to dream of a place you remembered. But your dreams were strange tonight. Darkness and faces..."

"I can try to show you something."

"It doesn't work that way. Once I enter your dream state, only I—"

Autumn ignored him, concentrating on the image of her paternal grandparents' home. The ancient city whispered away like smoke, and suddenly the two of them were standing in the living room of a small Chicago bungalow. The walls were wood-paneled, and the shag carpet beneath their feet was some indeterminate color between green and brown. Kitschy green owls hung above a red brick fireplace. The mustard yellow couch and armchair were patterned with orange and brown flowers.

Irdu blinked. "How did you—?" He stared at their surroundings. "You shouldn't be able to do this!"

"You also said I shouldn't be able to remember you, and that I shouldn't be able to break the dream state, and look at us now."

Irdu's expression turned speculative. "You're... different. In every way."

Autumn smiled, pleased. "Come on, I'll show you my grandma and grandpa's house." She took him on a tour of a house she hadn't seen in more than a decade. She brought him to the kitchen and showed him where her grandma had always stored black and white duplex cookies in a glass cookie jar above the fridge. She showed him the upstairs closet that she used to turn into a fort with blankets and pillows. She brought him to the bedroom she'd always slept in when she spent the weekend at Grandma and Grandpa's. She bounced happily onto the twin bed, snatching up the colorful afghan blanket and wrapping it around her shoulders.

Irdu eased down next to her. He looked around the small room—at Grandma's collection of ceramic cats on the bookshelf, the crate of 45s next to the record player, a framed poster of Elvis, the stuffed animals clustered on the bed.

He picked up one of the stuffed animals, a purple monkey she'd named Gulliver. "What were you like as a child?" he asked.

"Happier," Autumn said. "I always liked art. I was always drawing. I liked animals a lot. I used to think I wanted to be a

vet." She glanced at him, at the careful way he handled her mangy old stuffed animal. "What were you like?"

He was quiet for a moment. He set Gulliver back amongst the other stuffed animals. "I don't remember much. My parents were... farmers, maybe? Not the owners of a farm, but laborers. Perhaps slaves."

Autumn leaned against him, offering silent comfort.

"I remember my father's death. I was young enough that I didn't understand the seriousness of the situation until long after, when I finally realized that he was gone. Forever."

Autumn wrapped her arms around him. "I'm sorry you've been dealt such a horrible hand. I wish I could—"

—save you. But she didn't say it out loud. Tomorrow she would get some answers. She'd figure something out.

Irdu turned to her. "It hasn't been horrible. Not lately." He kissed her gently. He looked at her, his expression inscrutable. He leaned in and kissed her again, deeper, longer. Gently, he eased her onto her back.

"Not under my grandma's roof!" Autumn gasped as his lips trailed down her throat. "If she saw you getting frisky with her granddaughter, she'd whack you with the big ladle!"

Irdu continued kissing his way across her collarbone. "Let me be with you like this—as a man instead of a monster."

Autumn touched his cheek, tried to make him look her in the eye. "You're not a monster," she said fervently.

He took her mouth again, kissing her into wordless acquiescence. When he broke away, they were both breathing hard. "Do you accept the covenant of fornication?" he asked.

Autumn drew back, concerned. "Why are you asking this again?"

"I have to in the dream state."

She regarded him for a moment. She didn't like the hollowness in his eyes. She'd do anything to take it away. "I accept."

They undressed each other slowly, kissing and tasting every inch of bared skin. Autumn traced her fingers and lips over his warm, human skin—deeply bronzed, and bare of tattoos or piercings. She kissed a mouth that lacked fangs. She ran her fingers through curling hair uninterrupted by horns. When his eyes glazed with lust, they remained a warm, rich brown. The physical differences disarmed her, but she gave herself over to him as fully as ever.

They moved together with familiar ease, hips rocking together as his body entered hers. She wrapped her arms around him and held him close as he drove into her, trying to touch him everywhere, hold him as tightly as she possibly could.

"Irdu, Irdu..." she chanted his name with the reverence of prayer, trying to convey to him how much he—whether human or demon—meant to her. She wanted him to lose himself in her. That he wanted her for his own needs, independent of her desire, filled her with a chaotic swell of emotions—pleasure, love, pride, hope.

His thrusts came more erratically, and suddenly he shuddered and buried himself deep inside of her, and she felt the hot flood of his release. The pleasure of it brought her to her own climax and they gasped and arched together in the throes of it.

Later, he lay beside her, stroking her hair, staring distantly.

"You came before I did," Autumn said.

"That can't be..." He continued to stare.

"You did. I felt it."

"I..." He shook his head. Giving up on words, he pulled Autumn tightly to him. They lay together in stunned, sated silence, feeling the pound of their hearts.

AUTUMN WOKE TO THE SOUND OF HER ALARM. SHE was still in Irdu's arms, just as she'd been in their dream. She reached up to touch his cheek, stroke her thumb across his lip. She felt the point of one fang.

"Good morning," he said, lips moving against her fingers. He reached over her, grabbed her phone, and turned off the alarm. "You set it earlier than yesterday," he said, sounding surprised.

"I want more than a few minutes with you. The days are getting longer—sunrise comes a little earlier every morning, and sunset comes a little later every night."

They lay together in pleasant silence. The events of the dream weighed heavy in Autumn's mind. He'd come on his own, without her orgasm pushing him over. Did that mean anything? Or were the rules of the dream state different than physical reality?

When the sky began to lighten, Autumn clung tightly to Irdu. "Don't leave," she whispered.

Irdu touched her cheek. "I have to."

And then he was gone. Autumn was alone in her bed, tangled in blankets that still radiated Irdu's warmth. She sat up slowly, wearily.

"I think I love you," she whispered to the empty room.

Chapter Eight

"So, the thing about Inanna's Descent into the Underworld, is that it's commonly misread as a story of triumph over death, and a celebration of the power of Inanna, a goddess of life-affirming qualities like sex."

Dr. Leila Kader sat across from Autumn at a little cafe table. She paused to take a drink of her latte before continuing.

"But it's actually a demonstration of the Underworld's power and the irrevocability of certain consequences. Inanna dies when she enters the Underworld. She's only saved because her father—the most powerful god in the pantheon—intervenes. And even once she's revived and escaped the Underworld, another must take her place—another god. In this story, even gods cannot totally thwart death. So really, Inanna's Descent into the Underworld is not an adventure story about an intrepid heroine escaping death. It's about an entitled bitch who got what was coming to her because she thought she was above the consequences."

Autumn's hopeful bubble burst. "Oh," she said heavily.

"Sorry, excuse my language. I get in the habit of livening up lectures—"

Autumn waved away her apology. "I'm not offended. It's just that this interpretation really defeats the point of my project."

"Oh, that's right. Liz said you're an artist. You're doing something involving Inanna?"

"Well, I was hoping to. I'm not really sure, now. Speaking of which..." Autumn reached into her bag and pulled out her sketchbook. She flipped to the page where she'd drawn Irdu's tattoos and handed it over. "Do these look like anything to you?"

"Hmm... interesting." Dr. Kader leaned over the sketchbook, examining Autumn's painstaking transcriptions of Irdu's tattoos.

"Is it cuneiform?" Autumn asked.

"Yes, it's definitely cuneiform." Leila adjusted her glasses, peering closer. "Early Akkadian, if I'm not mistaken."

"Can you read it?"

She touched one of the symbols. "This is the ideogram for 'night.'" She tapped another. "This is 'death.' Here we have 'slave.' And 'body.' A few of these I'm not certain about. This one could be 'man' but there appears to be some sort of modifier added onto it. And this one I'm not familiar with, but it looks similar to the ideogram for 'power.'" Leila's brows shot up. "Well, well. I believe this is the ideogram for the god Nabu."

Autumn went perfectly still. *Nabu.* The god for whom the tower in Borsippa had been built.

"And... strange. This is definitely the ideogram for Inanna." She frowned. "They're from the same pantheon, but you don't often see those two deities paired in Mesopotamian cosmology."

"Does it form a sentence?"

"I'd have to check it against some references. Can I take a photo?"

"Sure."

Leila brought out her phone and snapped a picture of Autumn's sketchbook page. "I'll look at these and get back to you."

"That'd be great. Thank you."

Leila handed the sketchbook back to Autumn and drained the last of her coffee. "Well, thanks again for listening to me go on. You can keep the books as long as you want."

Autumn scooped up the books Leila had brought for her—a primer on the Mesopotamian pantheon of gods, a collection of Mesopotamian myths, and Leila's dissertation on Inanna's descent into the Underworld. "Thank you so much for taking the time to meet with me. This is going to be really helpful."

"Of course. When you're done with your project, I'd love to see it."

"Oh. Right." Autumn cleared her throat. "Definitely. I'll let you know."

When she got home from work, she turned her key slowly, filled with a mixture of anticipation and fear. She nudged her door open and peered into the dim quiet of her apartment.

Irdu sat in the cozy chair next to her dresser, tail draped over his knee, flipping through one of her books. He looked up and smiled at her.

"You're home."

"Hello," she said, unable to keep the relief from her voice. She kicked off her shoes and bounded over to him. Easing onto the arm of the chair, she looked down at the book in his hands. It was a photography book entitled *Kinship.* The photographer had traveled the United States, taking candid portraits of families of all different compositions and definitions.

Irdu had the page open to a group of traveling circus performers sitting at a picnic table behind an aluminum trailer house. One man was on the tabletop, wearing a white undershirt and ripped jeans, doing a handstand on one hand with a cigarette clamped between his lips. A woman in a silk kimono and beat-up cowboy boots leaned over with a zippo to light his cigarette. The rest of their group looked on, smiling and laughing.

Autumn stared at the image, feeling her throat constrict. She pushed off the arm of the chair and picked her shoes back up. She stepped into them.

"What are you doing?" Irdu set the book aside.

"I'm taking you somewhere where there are other people."

His eyes went wide. "*What?*"

"You'll have to wear a hat. And a big coat. And... maybe some makeup?"

"I still won't look even remotely human."

"We'll go somewhere dark. A movie theater, maybe."

"You can't be serious. Autumn. Look at me. I will never be able to—"

Autumn grabbed her bag. "Wait here—I'll be right back."

"What are you—"

"Just wait here. Please?"

Irdu sighed. "I don't know what you're doing, but this isn't going to work."

"It will. I'm an artist, remember?"

"Even the greatest artists can't change reality," Irdu said wearily.

Autumn gave him a pitying look. "Aw, darling. That's exactly what we do." She whisked out the door and raced off into the night.

It took her precisely thirty-seven minutes to race to the strip mall four blocks away, burst into the Big and Tall menswear store, buy clothing, sprint down the strip to the drug store, buy a tube of color correcting makeup and foundation and a pair of sunglasses, pay for them, and race back to her apartment.

When she burst back in, Irdu was sitting in the chair, chin braced on his hand, looking agitated.

"Here!" She dumped the shopping bags on her bed and began rifling through them. "This stuff might be a little big on you, but it's better than too small." She plucked up a pair of cargo pants and tossed them at him. "You'll have to tuck your tail down one of the pants legs. Sorry they're not exactly the height of fashion. I was aiming for concealment rather than sophistication."

"Autumn." Irdu stepped beside her, looking as if he were searching for the words to let her down gently.

She spun to him, gripping his arms. "Please, Irdu? Just try. *Please?*"

He looked at her for a moment, his inhuman features set in a grim mask. After a moment, his shoulders sagged, and he sighed. "Fine. I'm not saying we will go anywhere, but I will wear the things you've brought."

"Thank you!" She spun back to the clothes, handing him a t-shirt and hoodie. "Put these on."

He looked askance at the heap of clothes, then with an air of long-suffering patience, began struggling into the pants.

"Been a while since you wore pants, huh?"

"I've never worn pants."

"What? Oh." Autumn remembered the draped robes everyone had worn when he'd taken her back to his time in a dream. "Huh. Well, maybe it'd be easier if you sat down."

Irdu sank to the edge of the bed and Autumn helped him work the pants legs over his feet. Since they had the elongated shape of an animal paw, they slid in fairly easily, though his claws snagged on the seams occasionally. When they got the pants to his knees, he stood, and Autumn helped him thread his tail down the left pant leg. He hoisted the waist up and looked down at his clothed legs, bemused.

"Okay. So, this is a zipper," Autumn said.

"I know what a zipper is."

"Do you know how to close it?"

He grasped the tab with two claws and pulled it up.

"Impressive," Autumn said with an eyebrow waggle.

"Don't patronize me," he said with cool dignity—then ruined it was a self-satisfied smirk.

Getting the t-shirt on over his horns wasn't terribly difficult. But the hoodie ended up tangled all over his head, with one drawstring looped around his left horn, and the hood twisted around the right. The rest of the sweatshirt dangled limply over his face. Only his vivid blue eyes peered out from the neck hole, looking entirely unamused.

Autumn, on the other hand, was folded in half, barely able to breathe. "Oh my god—you look—you look—" She descended into a helpless fit of laughter.

Ignoring her, Irdu struggled with the sweatshirt on his own, but he was only making it worse.

"You have to stop!" Autumn gasped. She wiped at her streaming eyes, hauling in a desperate breath. "You're going to—"

Irdu snarled and tugged at the hoodie. He only managed to cover his face and tangle a sleeve around one horn.

"Ack!" Autumn fell to her knees, clutching her sides. "Going to—kill me!"

"Would you please get ahold of yourself and help me?" Irdu's voice came muffled through the cover of the hoodie.

"I'm sorry!" Autumn crawled forward, still hysterical, and

pulled herself up beside Irdu on the bed. Still apoplectic with laughter, she managed to clumsily work the sleeve free, then the drawstring. It took some more wrestling to work the hood over his horns, and when they'd finally gotten it pulled down around his neck, Irdu's face was flushed lilac and Autumn had managed to start breathing normally again.

"Note to self," Autumn said on a giggle. "Only zip-up hoodies for Irdu."

He looked down at himself. His clawed feet looked odd poking out of the bottom of his pants, and his clawed fingers weren't exactly human-like, but Autumn had bulky snow boots for his feet and mittens for his hands. But before they bothered with those, something needed to be done about his face.

She pulled him into the bathroom and made him sit on the toilet. The color-corrector she'd bought was for disguising the bluish hue of under-eye circles and wasn't meant to be spread over the whole face, but that was what she was going to do with it. It was a small tube, but Autumn had bought three of them, just in case.

Irdu sat patiently while Autumn daubed it over his face. When his face was evenly covered, she stepped back to survey the results.

"Not bad, actually," she said. "Once we put the foundation over the top, you'll totally pass for human." She used a big makeup brush to generously layer several coats of *Desert Sands* over his face and neck. When she was done, he was wearing enough foundation to paint a house. But the important part was that most people would look at his face and think, *somebody went overboard with the concealer,* instead of, *that dude is clearly not human.*

Autumn slid the sunglasses onto his face and stepped back again. He looked a little bit like a cadaver prepared for a funeral by a second-rate mortician. But he looked like a *human cadaver*, which was key.

Irdu got up and looked at himself in the mirror. He was quiet for several long seconds. Finally, he said, "If it weren't for the horns, this could actually work."

"You underestimate me, sir!" Autumn caught his hand and dragged him back out to the living area. She pushed him to sit on the bed and picked up a black slouchy knit hat.

"That will look absurd," he said.

"There are several layers to this solution, Donnie Doubter." She worked that hat over his head. It stretched between his horns, forming a large, wooly crest across the top of his head. It did look ridiculous. But she wasn't done. She grabbed the parka, and helped him into it, then flipped the hood up. The big, faux fur-lined hood covered his horns and hung down to his forehead.

"Go take a look," Autumn said, grinning broadly.

Irdu walked back to the bathroom. He was quiet again for a long time. Autumn went to the door and peered in.

"Well?"

"This may work," he said quietly.

"I know it will. Come on, I've got boots and mittens for you. The movie starts in half an hour."

"My hair is still blue." Irdu pointed to a few unruly locks poking out from under the hat.

"Every other teenager has rainbow colored hair these days. Nobody will think anything of it."

"My teeth?"

"Just pull your upper lip over the fangs."

Irdu stared at himself. He adjusted the sunglasses. Straightened the hood. Pulled his lip over his protruding fang tips. Stared some more.

"Alright," he said finally.

Autumn had bought snow boots with thick liners, hoping the voluminous padding would help with the unusual shape of his feet. He took a few practice steps. His gait was a bit odd, but nothing ridiculous.

Hand in mittened hand, they stepped outside together. Irdu stood on the sidewalk, looking around. Autumn's block was filled with old Polish flats. The big front windows were lit, revealing the movements of their inhabitants—watching television, wrestling with their kids, making dinner, petting their dogs, and in one elderly man's case, doing naked calisthenics.

Irdu's hand tightened on Autumn's.

"Come on," Autumn said, tugging him along the sidewalk. It was a twenty-minute walk to the budget cinema. They passed people on the sidewalk, who barely spared Irdu a glance. Those who did mostly seemed bemused by the guy wearing sunglasses at night. Irdu stared wonderingly at each passing person.

"I can't believe this." His hand had begun to tremble in hers. "I can't... I can't believe it."

Autumn's heart swelled until she felt likely to choke on it.

When they reached the cinema, Irdu froze in front of the doors, pulling his hand out of Autumn's. "I don't think I can do this," he said rigidly.

"You can. We passed a bunch of people on the street and they didn't react at all."

"But it's dark out. There's so much light in there!"

"Only the lobby is lit up. Just stand behind me. I'll do all the talking so that your fangs don't show—you need to pull your lip down again, by the way."

"I—I can't."

Autumn grabbed his hand. "Yes you can. Please? For me?"

Irdu's shoulders sagged. He let out a heavy sigh. "Yes. Alright."

"Okay." Autumn kept his hand and pulled the first set of

doors open. Irdu's hand squeezed hers like a vise. She led him through the next set of doors. The bored teenager at the ticket kiosk didn't even look up at them. Autumn collected their tickets and pulled Irdu quickly past concessions and into the dark of their theater.

"You're really big," Autumn said, leading him to the back row. "We'll sit here so we don't block anyone's view." Plus, if they were behind everyone, nobody would be able to look at him too much.

Autumn had to show Irdu how to flip the seat down. After sitting for a few seconds, he began to shift uncomfortably.

"What's wrong?" Autumn asked.

"My tail," he whispered. He shifted more aggressively, kicking one leg like he had a squirrel in his pants. After a minute he let out a little sigh and eased back.

"Alright?"

He caught her hand, folded it in his. "Yes."

As more people filtered into the theater, Irdu straightened. He watched their movement with total absorption. Autumn smiled to herself and settled back in her seat.

Autumn couldn't remember anything about the movie. She spent the whole time watching Irdu from the corner of her eye. She'd bet he didn't remember anything about the movie either. His head had turned slowly as he scanned the theatre. Little movements kept pulling his attention—a couple giving each other a little kiss, two friends squabbling over their shared popcorn, an old man shushing noisy teenagers, a woman checking her phone.

When the movie ended and lights came up, Irdu started. He gazed around at the other people as they gathered their things and pulled on their coats.

"What'd you think?" Autumn asked.

"I don't know what to think."

"I'll try to come up with some other places to go. Bars can be kind of dim... we could find a quiet one and sit at a corner table. You'd have to order a drink for show. The only problem is, a lot of places have bouncers, and you don't have any ID. Plus, the hood and the sunglasses are going to make them suspicious. Maybe we could try a—"

Irdu kissed her. When he pulled back, the makeup had smudged from his lips, revealing a hint of blue. "You're lovely," he said, emotion making his voice tight.

"You're lovelier," she told him. She reached out and gently tucked his lip over the points of his fangs. The ushers were beginning to clean the theater, so Autumn pulled Irdu to his feet and they made their way out. He walked through the brightly lit lobby with less urgency this time, looking around with the same hypervigilant fascination as in the theater.

When they emerged onto the sidewalk, Irdu pulled her to a halt again. He let out a burst of shaky laughter and wrapped her in his arms for a lung-crushing hug. He kissed the top of her head, again and again.

"Get a room," a passerby groused.

"I think we will," he told the guy, looking thrilled beyond measure to be speaking to another person.

Autumn let out a shocked laugh. "Irdu!"

He grinned at her. The night was dark, but under the streetlights, she could see his fangs very clearly. Still smiling his wolfish smile, he took her hand, and began the walk back to her apartment.

Back home, Autumn helped him out of the clothes—it was a lot easier to pull the hoodie off than it was putting it on. In the bathroom, she helped him remove the makeup and handed him a towel after he'd washed his face. Still smiling, Irdu wiped his face, tossed the towel to the side and threw Autumn over his shoulder.

She gave a delighted shriek as he carried her to the bed and tossed her down. He stripped her clothes away with cheerful urgency, his eyes shifting to black as he peeled her panties down her legs. Autumn stared breathlessly.

That's his own desire, she thought, certain of it. She was definitely in the mood, but she hadn't yet reached that single-minded need that was once necessary to turn his eyes black. In fact, it was Irdu's passion that was stoking her own. Each fevered touch of his lips against her skin, each panting breath coasting over her neck and ear, each drag of claw tips down her flanks, had her rising higher and higher into the pull of Irdu's arousal. She was a passenger to his need, responding to his urges, following his desire.

When he finally slid inside of her, the need between them bordered on painful. Hand in hand, they surged together, driving higher and hotter until they tumbled into mindless ecstasy. A split second before Autumn let herself fall, she witnessed Irdu's surrender. Satisfied, she followed him. As the pleasure of climax coasted over and through her, Autumn fell abruptly from bliss into sharp awareness of the void pressing around her.

The faces were clearer this time, closer. They crowded against the blue veil surrounding her. A low murmur emanated from them—the buzz of infinite whispering voices, angry, sorrowful, beseeching. A slithering cold draft penetrated the protection of the blue haze. It curled sinuously around her body, so cold it burned.

She jerked away from the sensation, and back into physical reality with a sudden jolt. Her skin still burned where the invisible coldness had touched her. Irdu loomed over her, a contented smile on his face. His eyes had already returned to normal—no blue aurora, no infinite black.

"There she is," he said, his voice lazy with satisfaction.

This was new, too. It was the first time he'd recovered before her. She looked into his pleasure-softened gaze and the painful cold was all but forgotten. She looped her arms around his neck and rolled with him until they were cuddled together, laying on their sides.

"You came before I did," she said smugly.

"We came at the same time. As we always do."

Autumn shook her head. "You were just a split-second ahead of me. Like you were last night."

Irdu shook his head, but he said nothing. They lay in each other's arms, quiet, thoughtful. Irdu let out a heavy breath.

"I don't know what this means." He seemed to be conceding the point.

"Is there anybody you can ask? Is there some ancient tome of demon lore that I can check out at the library?"

"No, and no."

"Hmm."

They fell into a curious, but comfortable, silence. Autumn was beginning to drift to sleep when Irdu's voice rumbled in her ear, "I don't know how, but you've made everything different."

Heart glowing, she curled into him, and surrendered to sleep.

Chapter Nine

Autumn spent her lunch researching various Underworld descent myths. She read several different versions of the Persephone myth—from Hesiod, to Homer, to Virgil, to Ovid. She read about Orpheus's attempt to retrieve Eurydice from death, and Odysseus's visit to the Underworld in his effort to return home to his wife Penelope.

Lunch ended, and she wasn't even a quarter of a way through all the tabs she'd opened on various Underworld myths. She packed her things and sent her erstwhile manager an email letting him know she was taking a half-day. Before going home, she popped into the Big and Tall men's store again, and bought a zip-up hoodie that would fit Irdu.

Back at her apartment, with the sun still up, she continued her research. She read about the Old Norse afterlife, Hel, and the various deities and mortals who had journeyed there. She read translations of Old English poetry about Christ's "Harrowing of Hell" and the Eastern Orthodox Church's tradition about Lazarus's four days in Hell. She read the Finnish myth of Lemminkäinen in which a mortal man dies upon entering the

Underworld, but is retrieved and resurrected by his mother. She read about Obtala, a Yoruba resurrection deity. She learned about the Hindu myth of Yudhishthira's descent into Naraka. In Welsh myth, the hero Pwyll spent a year and a day as the ruler of the Otherworld, called *Annwn*. She spent a significant chunk of time combing through the details of Osiris's death, and Isis's efforts to resurrect him.

Autumn's brain was buzzing with a thousand different stories, but she began to piece together several patterns emerging from them all. Figures associated with fertility enter the Underworld and die there. They are saved by a loved one, who puts their pieces back together and resurrects them with life-giving food or drink. The underworlds, by whatever name, are always underground. Getting to them requires passage over rivers or walls.

She found another Mesopotamian myth, this one about a mortal entering the Underworld. In the Epic of Gilgamesh, Gilgamesh's companion Enkidu is killed by the gods as a punishment. There he sees the goddess Belet-Seri, also known as the Scribe of the Dead, who was one of the gods who took Inanna's place after Inanna was rescued by Enki.

A scribe goddess...who took the place of a sex goddess...in the underworld. Autumn tapped her chin, thinking. She grabbed her sketchbook and flipped to the page where she'd drawn Irdu's tattoos. She'd made little notes beneath each ideogram, based on the email Dr. Kader had sent her with full translations for all the characters.

Irdu wore Inanna's mark. But he also wore the mark of Nabu, a scribe god. He was a sex demon, whose skin was covered in writing. He'd been a mortal, enslaved and forced to construct Nabu's temple. But now he was an immortal, toiling in service to the Underworld.

Life. Sex. She touched the ideogram that meant *body*. She slid her finger from ideogram to ideogram, whispering the meanings as she touched upon them. *"Death... night... slave."*

She stared at the cuneiform drawings, willing them to make sense to her. But she couldn't pull them into any logical combination.

"Hello."

Autumn screamed and pitched right off the foot of her bed. When she scrambled upright, she found herself staring at a horrified Irdu.

"I'm sorry!" he said, reaching for her. "I didn't mean to frighten you!" He eased her back onto the bed and began a careful examination of her limbs. "Mortals are fragile," he said fretfully. "An infected cut. Stagnant drinking water. A blow to the head. A sharp—"

"I'm okay, Irdu. Really." She caught his hands, stopping his anxious search for fatal injuries. "I was just surprised. I completely lost track of time." She closed her computer and sketchbook, setting them both on the nightstand. With her secret research out of sight, she turned back to Irdu and put her arms around his neck, letting her body melt against his, soaking in his warmth and his strength.

"You're home earlier than the last couple nights," he observed, holding her as tightly as she held him.

"Yeah, I took a half day off of work."

"Are you feeling well?"

"I'm fine. I just didn't want to be at work." Not a lie. Guilt ate at her anyway.

"If you're well, then I'm glad to see you sooner than I'd expected." He kissed the top of her head.

She pulled back to meet his gaze. "Well, you'll see me early tomorrow, too. And the next day. It's Christmas Eve and Christmas, and I don't have to work."

Irdu smiled, but it was a little sad. "You'll be spending your Christmas with me?"

"Yes. And you're the best person I could spend it with."

He looked at her skeptically.

"I'm serious."

He took that in for a moment. His expression softened.

"Do you want to go out again? I got you a zip-up hoodie."

His frown was back. "Between the dreams I've inhabited and the television I've watched, I know that wealth is still a pressing concern in this world. I wouldn't want you to spend your funds on entertaining me. I'm happy as long as I'm with you. I don't need—"

"I know you don't. And let me assure you, I'm far from rich, but I can afford a hoodie and a few movie tickets. It makes me happy to go out into the world with you. It makes me happy that I can give that to you."

Irdu looked troubled. "You already give me too much. And I give you nothing."

Autumn didn't know how to put into words everything he gave her. Comfort. Peace. Affection. Companionship. Mind-blowing orgasms. Those things couldn't be measured in dollars and cents, could never be bought, could never be so easily and bloodlessly acquired as a sweatshirt or a movie ticket. She'd never felt as happy in someone else's presence as she did in Irdu's. She'd give away every last penny she had if she could keep him with her always.

"You give me so much," she said, the words completely inadequate. "Making it so you can go places with me isn't something I'm doing only for you. I'm selfish, and I want to be with you everywhere I can be. If the cost is a pair of pants, then I'm getting a major bargain, okay?"

Irdu pursed his lips, clearly not placated, but didn't press the issue.

"Can we go out?" Autumn asked. "If you want to, I mean."

He glanced at her, and the tension faded from his mouth. "Yes, alright."

With the zip-up hoodie, dressing him was much easier. She hid his blue skin beneath color-corrector and foundation, and hid his horns beneath a knit hat and flipped-up parka hood. He slid on the sunglasses and out the door they went. This time, Autumn took him to the public library. It was more brightly lit than the cinema, but less crowded.

Irdu was nearly incandescent with nervous energy. Somebody passed them in a narrow aisle, murmuring, "Excuse me." Irdu replied, "No problem," and then shot Autumn a look of such utter delight that she nearly melted into a puddle of happiness. They sat in the reading room and pretended to read books, while Irdu was actually watching the other people, and Autumn was watching Irdu.

When they returned home, his excitement translated itself into passion again, and he made her come twice with his talented tongue before she shoved him onto his back, straddled his hips, and sank down on his cock. Every orgasm brought her to the same infinite darkness—but it wasn't until Irdu was inside her, when his climax preceded hers once again, that the strange, painful cold leeched into the protective embrace of the dancing blue haze.

It coiled around her body like a constricting snake, burning her skin with ice cold pain.

When she came back to herself, Irdu had her pulled against his chest, murmuring sweetly as he kissed her cheek, her jaw, her nose, her brow, her lips. His warmth banished the pain of the cold, and she curled into the comfort of his presence.

～

CHRISTMAS EVE MORNING, AUTUMN WOKE IN IRDU'S arms. He kissed her forehead before he vanished with the sunrise. She rolled into the warm spot he'd left in the sheets and checked the time of the sunset on her phone. She did the math in her head—a little more than nine hours before she'd see him again. With a grumble, she got out of bed.

She didn't have much to do with herself. Her mother lived in another state. Her only available friend was in D.C. It was too depressing to spend the holiday sitting alone, eating cold takeout, and binge-watching a crappy sci-fi series. With a sigh, she went to the closet. Last year, in a failed attempt to cheer herself up, she'd bought Christmas decorations and tricked out her apartment. She wasn't sure if Irdu would care much about Christmas decor, but it might prove to him that she was happy to be with him during the holiday.

She assembled her tiny fake Christmas tree and put it on the dresser beside her TV, draping it with glittery golden garland and brightly colored glass ornaments. She would've liked to have a couple gifts beneath it, but she had nobody to give them to. She could give Irdu something, but she suspected it would upset him.

She tacked string lights around her window. Standing on a stool, she hung green and red tinsel garland in swags along the top of the walls. She put three little candle-shaped lamps in her window. She hung a fake pine bough wreath on her door, placed two ceramic reindeer on her nightstand, and hung a printed canvas of Norman Rockwell's *Santa at the Map* on her wall. With the remainder of the garland, she trimmed the edge of her kitchen counter and her door.

When she was done, she stood in the center of her apartment, taking it all in, and found that she did feel a happy little lift at the sight of it.

Then she realized that she still had more than five hours to kill before Irdu returned. Her good mood dimmed a little. With a sigh, she pulled out her computer and went back to the research she'd been doing yesterday. She learned that there was a term for stories about descending into the underworld: *katabasis*.

Using that, she combed through academic journals on folklore, mythology, comparative literature, and theology, reading article after article about katabasis stories. She was trying to find connections between fertility deities, literacy deities, and the underworld. But the vast divergence in interpretations and analyses left her with more questions than answers.

She wasn't even sure what kind of answer she was looking for. In all honesty, she was mostly hoping she'd happen upon some random bit of information that would pull everything together into a perfect *eureka*. Everything would become crystal clear—exactly what she needed to do to save Irdu. If she could just stumble across a perfectly researched, peer-reviewed paper entitled *All World Religions Agree: to free a demon from eternal enslavement, just follow these three easy steps!*

Defeated, she closed her computer. A glance at the time told her she still had three hours until sundown. Deciding that all the lovely Christmas decor needed good Christmas smells, she pulled on her coat and walked to the corner store.

When Irdu finally appeared, Autumn's cheek was streaked with flour, her sweater had a big oil stain, and her left hand had long pink burn mark across the top. She hovered over the stove, whisking vigorously at gravy that had gone a little lumpy Irdu took in the sight of her, a fond smile curling his lips.

"Been busy?"

"Yes," she told him brightly. "I thought we could have a

holiday dinner together. I know you said you *don't* eat, but *can* you eat?"

Irdu shrugged. "Probably. I'm not certain what would happen."

"Would it kill you?" Autumn looked up, clutching her whisk.

"No. But I might have to... er... regurgitate it."

"Oh. Then I won't ask you to eat anything. But you can keep me company while I eat my smorgasbord. I made my favorites—pumpkin pie, mashed potatoes with gravy, and my grandma's flaky biscuits."

"It sounds highly nutritious," he said dryly.

It was a bit carb-heavy, but those were the things she'd always loaded her plate with when she was a kid at family holidays. "Nutritional values are moot on holidays. Everyone knows that."

"You don't have a single vegetable on your plate."

"Excuse me, Judgey McJudgerson, but I have *pumpkin* pie and mashed *potatoes*. That'll be *two* vegetables on my plate."

He raised his eyebrows. She grinned unrepentantly and started scooping mashed potatoes onto her plate. "This is the way my dad made them," she said, creating a mountain. "Baby reds. Leave the skins on. In a separate pan, caramelize some onions. Then you mash the potatoes and onions together with roasted garlic, chives, salt and pepper, butter, and—the secret ingredient—cream cheese." She shoveled a spoonful into her mouth and sighed happily. "It's *so* bad for you."

"I've never eaten potatoes."

Autumn froze halfway through ladling gravy onto her potato mountain. "*What?*"

"Potatoes originated in the Americas. And I don't think they'd even been domesticated when I was human."

Autumn's eyes rounded. "Look, I don't want to pressure

you into bulimia, but these potatoes are worth the possibility of having to regurgitate them later."

Irdu eyed them unenthusiastically. "Forgive me, but they look a great deal like plaster."

Autumn pulled out a second plate and began filling it with small portions of everything. "Just try a little nibble, see what you think."

"I'm not certain I have the ability to taste food."

"Can you taste me?"

Irdu's gaze darkened, fixing on her with a predatory gleam that made her flush. "Let me see." He rounded the kitchen counter, tilted her chin up, and kissed her long and deep. His tongue swept into her mouth as his fangs pressed her lips. When he pulled away, Autumn realized she'd dripped gravy all over the stovetop.

"Well?" she asked, a little breathless.

"Yes. I taste you. But you are living flesh, filled with the energy that sustains me. And this..." he glanced at the mashed potatoes and failed to find an adequate finish to his sentence.

"Well, just give it a tiny little try." Autumn brought their plates to the counter. She pulled out both stools and gestured for Irdu to come sit beside her. As he settled skeptically into his seat, she nudged a fork towards him, and waited eagerly.

He picked it up awkwardly. His claws wouldn't allow him to grasp a fork the way she did, so he was forced to hold it in a clenched fist. Taking just the barest little dab of potato, he reluctantly put it into his mouth.

After a moment, he shrugged. "It didn't taste like anything."

"Because you ate a single potato molecule. Take a bigger bite."

Sighing, he took a more reasonable portion, and put it in his mouth. His jaw worked, then his throat. When he looked back at Autumn, he shrugged. "I can taste the flavors you told me about. But they don't give me the pleasure that they give you."

Autumn frowned. The logical side of her brain acknowledged that a creature who didn't need to eat to survive would not get pleasure from eating, but something emotional and stubborn compelled her to make him enjoy a meal with her. "Try the biscuit. It's spread with garlic butter."

Irdu complied, taking a modest bite, chewing, and swallowing. "I'm sorry, Autumn. I'm sure it's lovely to humans. But it's a wasted experience on me."

"I know. I don't know why I'm being stubborn about this." She poked unhappily at her own plate. "Would you try the pumpkin pie, anyway? Just for the sake of closure?"

The corner of his mouth quirked up, and he took a good-natured bite of the pie.

"Thank you," she told him. "Sorry for being pushy." She tucked into her own plate, moody and thoughtful.

"You said these are your father's potatoes, and your grandmother's biscuits. Are they traditional for you?" Irdu asked, poking at the food on his plate.

"Yeah. We always used to spend Christmas Day with my dad's family, at Grandma and Grandpa's house—the house I showed you in the dream."

"It was a safe harbor for you?"

"I spent most weekends at Grandma and Grandpa's when I was little. All the big holidays were at their house. After Dad died, I ended up living with them for a while when Mom turned into a zombie. Grandma and Grandpa were always good to me. Thinking about them and their home always makes me happy."

Irdu touched her cheek. "Thank you for bringing me there."

"I'm glad you saw it." Feeling cheered, she ate her Holiday Carbs with more zeal. To her utter shock, Irdu attempted another bite of the potatoes. Unsure what to say—but certain that she didn't want to hear again about how the taste of them was meaningless—she chose to pretend she hadn't noticed.

Irdu asked her about her family's holiday traditions. She asked him about holidays from the time of his human life, and he struggled to remember them, describing bits and pieces of different festivals and celebrations. Here and there, he took little tastes from his plate, seemingly unaware of doing it. Autumn followed each bite with laser focus.

That night, when they came together in bed, Irdu eased back from her, holding her in place. "I have a gift for you," he said in a husky voice.

"You got me a Christmas present? But I didn't—"

"*Shhh.*" He kissed her silent. "I've been thinking about this for a while, and I'd like to try it tonight. I think I can rebound the sexual energy I harvest back to you."

"What? No! You'll die if you don't have enough."

"I'll keep as much as I need. If I return the excess to you, that's less energy I take back to the Underworld, and the less I further the Host's goals."

Autumn relaxed. "Okay. Let's try it. What do I have to do?"

Irdu gave her a wicked smile and hoisted her legs over his shoulders. "Just enjoy yourself."

When she came, clutching both of Irdu's horns while his face was buried between her thighs, she felt her own pleasure, and then a surge of power rolled through her. Like a rolling blackout, it spread from the core of her body outwards, taking every sense offline until she was plunged into utter darkness.

And then everything exploded. She was a being of pure sensation—no thought, no emotion, just total, unadulterated pleasure.

But alongside the pleasure, a shadow loomed. It twined around her, insinuating itself into the goodness. Spikes of pain radiated through her, flashing hot and cold. The darkness flickered and strobed. She was surrounded by hollow-eyed faces, and then she wasn't. The darkness began to resolve into shapes and figures, fading in and out of visibility. As the cold constriction intensified around her, the shapes came into focus—a massive, sprawling city.

Smoky, dark, crumbling buildings spidered and sprawled across a jagged, craggy landscape of broken black rock split with deep, irregular fissures. In the very center—a tower. Made of blocks of black stone, a mass of bodies toiled across its every surface like ants on a mound. Fire belched from forges at the tower's base. Demonic overseers circled the tower on leathery black wings. From inside the tower, an insidious power radiated —the source of the cold that was twining even tighter around Autumn, sinking into her...

"Autumn!"

She snapped abruptly back to herself. Irdu was clutching her arms, staring down at her with wide-eyed alarm.

"Irdu?"

"Are you alright?" He ran his hands frantically over her body, peering into her eyes, listening for her heartbeat.

"I think so." She pushed herself up, feeling bruised and achy.

"What happened? What did you feel?" Irdu asked urgently, anxiously propping pillows behind her.

She'd seen the Underworld. She knew it with the same certainty that told her there was a way to save Irdu. He was trapped in servitude to another tyrant—building yet another tower.

"I'm alright," she told him. "I didn't expect such... an experience."

"It was too much. I'm so sorry. I wasn't thinking. I just wanted to give you something—"

She pressed her fingers gently to his lips. "It wasn't too much." She needed to see it again—needed to figure out how to get him out of there for good. Academic publications and Wikipedia articles weren't cutting it. She needed to understand the real thing. "It was an excellent gift."

Even though she'd *just* had the wildest orgasm of her life, she felt an acute need to repay the favor. She wanted to make Irdu come, and she wanted to make him do it without depending on her pleasure for it. They'd proven he could come before her—now she wanted to see if he could come without bringing her with.

She broke away from the pillow nest Irdu had built around her and crawled onto Irdu, using her weight to drive him onto his back. He blinked up at her, perplexed.

"Now *I* have a gift for *you*," she told him, and began kissing her way down his chest.

"Autumn, this isn't necessary." He reached for her, tried to lift her head, but she swatted his hands away.

"No touching," she told him in a silky growl.

He flushed high on his cheekbones, his skin darkening to dusky lavender. His expression was equal parts bewildered and aroused. He liked when she took control. He'd told her as much, in subtler ways—insisting he belonged to her, and making her say it. So, she used it against him.

"You're mine." Her tongue slid over the golden barbell piercing in one nipple. A faint tremor ran beneath his skin, and she felt it in her lips. "You'll do as I say, because you want to please me. Isn't that right?" She brought her lips to his other nipple and flicked her tongue over the peaked nub. When he didn't answer her, she bit him.

His back arched, lifting her with his body. *"Ah!"* He gasped. *"I'm yours!"*

Appeased, she licked the spot she'd bitten, and continued tasting her way down his body. When she reached his cock, he was hard and ready. The three big barbells studding the underside of his shaft beckoned to her tongue. She tasted each one individually, and with each one, Irdu trembled and writhed.

"How are you doing this to me?" he gasped.

Autumn merely smiled. She wasn't completely unaffected, but between the two of them, Irdu was the one being driven mad. Remembering his reaction last time she'd played with his piercings, she gently closed her teeth around the top one, and tugged. Irdu's hips bucked, and he let out a low, fevered moan. He gripped the sheets with clenched fists.

"Do you like that?" Autumn asked.

"Yes." His breath was coming in desperate pants, his hips flexing in minute, measured thrusts.

Gripping the base of his cock, Autumn took the piercing between her teeth and tugged again, harder this time. Irdu groaned desperately, his hips thrusting, his erection pulsing hotter and harder. Autumn licked the tender skin she'd just tormented, and then licked up to his shining purple crown. She took him into her mouth with soft, wet suction. Irdu's hips bucked, pushing him deeper into her mouth. She allowed it, taking him to the back of her throat, using her hands to grip the extra inches she couldn't manage to take in.

"Ah!" Irdu writhed beneath her. "Autumn! What—I can't —" His words died on an incoherent groan as she began to work up and down his shaft, licking and sucking and squeezing. She trailed gentle fingers over his testicles, teasing and caressing. She felt them tighten against his body, and when she thought he was close to the edge, she released him from her mouth.

He let out a desperate moan, sagging back against the mattress.

"Whose are you?" Autumn asked.

"Yours!"

She advanced along his body until she straddled his hips. Gripping his shaft, she guided him to her slick, swollen folds. Sinking down, she took his length inside her with a satisfied sigh. Working her hips, she rode him slowly at first, slowly gaining speed. Irdu's back arched, his jaw clenched, fangs bared, fists still clenched in the sheets. At last, he couldn't take it anymore. Autumn felt his climax tear through him.

And then, to her utter shock, she felt something else—the warm, hot spill of his seed deep inside her. It was a delicious, intoxicating heat. It intensified, spreading through her whole body in wave after wave of brilliant pleasure. For the second time, Autumn felt herself plunge away from the constraints of her physical body and drop abruptly into complete and utter darkness.

The endless black resolved more quickly this time, revealing the tower again. This time she was closer. She could see sparks flying from the red-hot glow of the forges. She could see the demonic faces of the builders, creased with agony, rigid with terror, as they labored beneath the other demons' vicious watch. The frigid evil emanating from the tower cut through Autumn like a knife, stealing all of her pleasure and replacing it with painful emptiness. The tower loomed larger and larger, the cold becoming deeper and sharper. Through a window, she saw a figure—a naked woman, with ice white hair and eyes that gleamed like cut diamonds. Those eyes flicked to Autumn, held her gaze.

They were utterly inhuman, and filled with a power beyond Autumn's comprehension. The force of the woman's gaze ate at her like acid. She felt herself disintegrating away to nothing.

But then she remembered why she was here, why she needed to see the tower and its sinister occupant.

Irdu.

She shuttered her gaze and pulled his face to her mind. Irdu, she whispered in her mind. *Irdu... Irdu...*

"Irdu!"

Her eyes flew open, and she was back with him. He was still inside her, still shuddering through the last tremors of his orgasm. The powerful warmth of his orgasm still resonated inside of her. She slid off of him and pressed her fingers between her thighs. Instead of coming away sticky with semen, they were wreathed in a blue smoke that dissipated quickly.

"That's... strange."

Irdu lay beside her, still looking an absolute wreck. For a brief moment—so quickly she could have imagined it—his skin flashed to the tan shade he'd shown her in her dreams. His human skin. Autumn did a double-take, but by then, he was back to his cuneiform-marked blue skin.

Finally, Irdu seemed to be regaining his wits. He lifted his head weakly, stared at her, and then dropped it back down. Autumn stretched out beside him, stroking his hair while he recovered.

"Are you alright?" she asked.

"I—without—shouldn't have..." He shook his head and stared up at the ceiling. He laughed, and then he groaned. "I don't know what we've done," he said, his words shaky and slurred. "I don't know what this means."

It means I'm saving you. "Just relax. Do you want some water, or something?"

"I don't need water," he said. "You know that."

"Not usually..."

He blinked at her. "I...yes. Maybe some water would..." He shook his head again and let out an incredulous laugh.

Hiding a manic grin, Autumn went to the kitchen and filled a glass of water. It took her a second to get her face under control before she could return to him. She handed him the glass of water and watched with nervous hope. He took one small sip, then another. After a moment's hesitation, he drained the entire glass.

"That was... *good*." He stared at the empty glass. "It felt *good* to drink water!" He looked up at her as if he'd forgotten she was there for a second. "*Autumn*," he said heavily. "You're... you're..." He went back to staring at the glass.

"Are you alright?" Autumn asked gently.

"I think so," he said faintly.

"Okay. Good." She gently prized the glass from his grip and set it on the nightstand. "So, we should probably talk about what just happened."

"I don't even know where to begin."

"Let's begin with the biggest surprises—you came without me. And you ejaculated... sort of. And I think I took some kind of... energy, maybe... from it. And it made me come. I think we did some sort of switcheroo."

Irdu sat bolt upright, his expression stark with horror. "No. *No.* That can't be!"

"Irdu, it's alright, calm down."

"You don't understand!" He caught her by the shoulders, looking urgently into her eyes. "I told you—there is a way for me to escape my bondage. Do you remember?"

Autumn froze. "Somebody else has to take your place."

"I *will not* let that happen to you." His grip became painful, claw points sinking into her skin. "I will let myself dissipate before I'll—"

"No!" Autumn nearly screamed. "Promise me you won't do that. Now. Promise me you'll never—"

"I can't make that promise."

"You told me you'd give me everything!"

"Yes. And if I have to give my life—meaningless as it has been until you—then I will do so."

"Irdu, no!" Tears welled in her eyes. "Listen, that's not what's happening. I'm not taking your place." Even as she spoke the words, she knew they were lies. Why else had she been seeing the Underworld when he gave her pleasure?

He looked at her sadly. "I can't risk it, love."

"There's some other explanation." She cast around frantically, trying to come up with something. "Maybe when you tried to return some of sexual energy back to me, we opened up a new pathway. One that runs in both directions. Now I can take from you, and you can take from me."

Irdu's expression blanked. He went perfectly still. Autumn could see thoughts racing behind his eyes. Suddenly, he grabbed Autumn's shoulders and hauled her towards him for a wet, smacking kiss. He let out a shaky laugh. "Of course. I haven't done any of the ritual for exchanging souls, so it must be something else. A new connection." He laughed again, sounding a little hysterical.

"There's a ritual?" Autumn asked. "How does it go?"

"I'm not telling you."

"But what if some other demon comes along and tries to trick me into exchanging my soul? Shouldn't I know what to look out for?"

Irdu's brows lowered, a dark line over brooding eyes. He let out a sigh. "Don't let a demon feed you. Ever."

But what happens if I feed a demon? she wondered, but didn't dare voice it aloud. He'd start talking about dissipating himself again.

"And never let them mark you. Not a drawing, a tattoo, anything."

What about bite marks?

"And never give them your full name."

Do I know your *full name? Are you just* Irdu, *or is there more you haven't told me?* "You know my full name."

"But I haven't done anything with it. I've never called you by it."

"What would happen if you called me by my full name?"

"Nothing, because I wouldn't have any intention of using it for ill purposes." He looked disgusted with himself, holding the end of his tail in that nervous way that he did when they'd first met each other.

Autumn leaned forward and plucked his tail out of his hands. She stroked her fingers through the tufted end. "I trust you. I know you would never hurt me." She bit the tip of his tail playfully and grinned when he jumped. "So, if I just harvested sexual energy from you, thanks to our new two-way road, does that mean your tank is empty? I don't want to send you away without the energy you need."

Irdu's gaze was hesitant. "I... yes. I can feel that you've depleted me."

Her grin spread. "I'm that good?"

Irdu's hesitancy gave way to a fond smile. "The best I've ever known."

She gave his tail a little tug. "Then come here and return the favor."

Chapter Ten

When Autumn woke the next morning, the rising sun was casting long fingers of light through her window. Beside her, a brown-skinned, black-haired man lay in her bed, asleep.

She'd never seen Irdu asleep. The sight was more alarming than seeing him in human skin. It suddenly occurred to her that she was seeing him in... *daylight*. Her eyes grew round. She reached out to touch him, certain she must be dreaming. But before she could lay a finger on him, his skin melded back into tattooed blue. His horns and fangs reappeared. His eyes blinked open, met hers, and then he was gone.

Autumn bolted up and went to the window. The sky was pale blue, with no hint of predawn darkness. She scrambled for her phone, looking up the time of sunrise for the day, then checking it against the actual time.

He'd stayed eleven minutes past sunrise.

. . .

Autumn spent the day cooking, waiting for Irdu's arrival.

Bare minutes before sundown, there was a knock at her door. She nearly jumped out of her skin at the sound. Her building had an intercom system. Anybody coming by would have to buzz her unit from outside so she could let them in. Making it extra weird, there was nobody in town who'd want to come by except for maybe Liz. But it was Christmas day and Liz was with her family.

Wiping flour from her hands, Autumn went to the door and peered through the peephole. She physically recoiled.

Dylan.

She stood at the door, frozen. Part of her wanted to stand in silence until he left. The other part wanted to rip the door open and scream obscenities at him. After a moment, she managed to accomplish a compromise between the two—she wrenched the door open and stared at him without speaking.

"Hi, Autie." He gave her a wounded smile.

"Don't call me that."

He straightened. "Sorry."

An uncomfortable silence lapsed. Dylan looked as good as he ever had—better, even. Tall and lean, he was dressed in rich-guy casual—a dark green cashmere sweater over a chambray shirt, with perfectly fitted jeans and immaculate white sneakers, all topped by a tailored black coat. His thick, auburn hair was beautifully cut and artfully tousled. His beard was growing in better than it used to, the cheeks finally filled in, and all of it neatly groomed.

Autumn, on the other hand, was wearing a frayed Green Bay Packers sweater and bleach-stained leggings. Her hair was piled on top of her head into a messy topknot and she didn't have a lick of makeup on. She'd been planning to change quickly and let her hair down before Irdu arrived—the thought of which sent her into a wild panic. Irdu was due to appear any minute. What would happen when a giant blue demon manifested in the middle of her tiny apartment, right before Dylan's eyes?

"I'm really not interested in seeing you," Autumn said coldly, pushing the door shut.

"Wait, Autumn, just give me a second." Dylan caught the door. He didn't step into the apartment, but he didn't let her shut him out either. "A few people have told me things have been rough for you since we broke up, and I wanted to come by and make sure you were alright."

Autumn pushed against the door, but Dylan's strength outmatched hers. Giving up, she let the door swing open. At this point, she *wanted* Irdu to appear in front of Dylan. She'd love to see him scream. "How the hell did you get into my building?"

"Your neighbor was coming in when I walked up, and she held the door for me. Listen, I regret how things—"

"How do you know where I live?"

"I've kept tabs on you, Autumn. I still care about you. You were a big part of my life. You were there when I was nobody. You were by my side when I became *somebody*."

"You have money, so now you're somebody? Glad to know I can add *shallow* and *greedy* to your list of faults."

Instead of taking offense, Dylan smiled warmly at her. "Always so principled. I used to think of you as the 'good angel' on my shoulder."

Autumn glared at him, confused and agitated. "Why are you here? Is this some Ghost of Christmas Past bullshit? If you're looking for forgiveness, I don't have any."

"I just... I want to help you." He looked around her tiny apartment, his gaze lingering pityingly on the bed, mere feet from the kitchen, shoved up against a frost-glazed window.

"I don't want your help, Dylan. I want you to leave."

"Can we please talk? Just for a few minutes?"

"No."

"Fine. I'll just say one thing. Leaving you was the biggest mistake of my life."

"Actually, Dylan, *I* left *you*. You were perfectly happy to keep me while you were fucking other people."

He winced. "I've had a lot of time to think about the mistakes I've made. If you think you can ever forgive me, I'll do everything in my power to win you back."

She wasn't expecting *that*. "What?"

"I ended things with Alesandria."

"Did she catch you cheating on her, too?"

Dylan's repentant expression flickered to annoyance. "Still a ballbuster, I see."

"Careful with the compliments. I'll swoon."

"It *was* a compliment. I always liked your toughness."

Autumn didn't have a snappy response for that one. That had been one of the nice things about Dylan—he had genuinely seemed to like that she was stubborn and blunt. He'd once told her that his favorite pastime was watching her argue with idiots.

"Listen, I know you're not going to forgive me overnight. I took way too long to reach out, way too long to apologize, and way too long to come to my senses. But I know you're still working at that sham foundation—"

"None of your fucking business."

"—and I know you're not dating anyone."

"I *am* actually dating someone," she said primly.

Dylan looked staggered. "What?" His expression transformed to anger. "Who is he?" The anger cooled to suspicion. "If you're seeing someone, why isn't spending Christmas with you?"

"He had to work today," Autumn lied easily. "He's going to be here any minute, so if you wouldn't mind?" She shooed him back, but he wouldn't be moved.

"If you can forgive me Autumn, I'll spend my entire life trying to make it up to you. I want you back in my life. Anything you want, I'll give to you. You can have your job back at Apollo Tech. I'll get you a better place than this—your own place—while we work things out. Clothes, jewelry, cars, whatever you want."

Autumn's expression hardened. "You didn't used to be the kind of man who thought he could buy women."

He sighed. "Most people can be bought, Autumn. I wasn't trying to insult you. I just want... I want you back."

"I want you to leave."

Dylan stared at her, genuine grief writ across his features. Finally, he pushed away from the door. "I'll... I'll be in touch. Merry Christmas, Autie."

A lump rose in her throat at Dylan's old nickname for her. She closed the door without responding.

When she turned around, Irdu was standing behind her. She nearly jumped out of her skin. "Irdu!" She clapped her hand over her racing heart. "When did you get here?"

"A few minutes ago."

"What! Did Dylan see you?"

"No. I couldn't fully materialize while he was here."

"You heard the whole conversation."

"Yes." He was fiddling with the end of his tail.

Autumn crossed the distance between. She pulled his tail from his hands and wrapped her arms around him. "Hug me," she said, pressing her face into his chest.

His arms came around her, strangely perfunctory. "He can offer you everything you need," Irdu said in a hollow voice.

Autumn pulled back from him. "Everything I need?" she

repeated, feeling her hackles rise. "Are you telling me to take him back?"

"He can give you gifts. He can take you anywhere. He can be with you in the daylight. He has money. A great deal of money, from the sound of it."

Anger and sadness warred in Autumn's chest. "I don't need to be *given* anything!" she snapped. "What I *need* is somebody who treats me well, who makes me happy, and who appreciates me. If I wanted money from him, I'd go after him for never paying me for all the designs I did for his company."

Irdu's expression jumped from resignation to astonishment. "He owes you money?"

"Not really. Well. Sort of. I mean, it's not like there's an itemized invoice that he's refusing to pay. When he was just starting out, he was getting nowhere. So I designed a website and did all the corporate branding for his company. It was a tiny company then. And I did it to be a supportive girlfriend, not to make a buck. But, since there was never any kind of financial exchange, he technically never bought the rights from me, so I hold all the copyrights on the designs. Which Apollo Tech is still using, even after he hired a new brand manager." She shrugged. "I could probably demand payment. Shortly after we broke up, I started looking into it, but then I realized I was only acting out of bitterness. If we were still together, I'd never have asked to be paid."

"Which would have been understandable when you were sharing the life that you built together," Irdu said, brows drawing together. "But you're no longer sharing that life. You deserve to have your portion of what you built."

"If I go after him, I'm just going to look like a scorned woman trying to get back at her ex."

"He deserves your scorn. He's a snake and he used you.

He's living the high life off your work. He owes his success to that work. And you're just going to let him walk away with it?"

"He doesn't owe his success to me. He owns a software company, and he's a computer scientist. I'm just someone with a good eye for color."

Irdu scowled. "You told me weeks ago that his company didn't take off until you improved all the visuals."

Autumn shrugged. "He's succeeding because his product is excellent. I just made it so people noticed the product and took it seriously."

"And you deserve to be compensated for doing that."

"I don't disagree with you. But we're just back to my original point—regardless of what's fair or true, public perception will still be that I'm a gold-digger trying to stick it to my wealthy, successful ex."

Irdu caught her by the shoulders, looking furiously into her eyes. "So what, Autumn? The public can choke on their self-righteous idiocy. At least you'll get the credit—and the money —you deserve."

She sighed. "Even if I wanted to, I can't afford the kind of lawyers that would have any hope of taking on Dylan's legal team."

"Find a lawyer who'll work on contingency."

Autumn regarded him skeptically. "Are you a sex demon or a legal expert?"

Irdu smiled. "I've been around for a long time, love. I know a thing or two about humans. Until I met you, I had a lot of spare time to spend reading, observing, and learning."

Autumn batted her eyelashes coquettishly. "Oh, I'm sorry, have I been keeping you from your studies? However shall I make it up to you?"

Irdu grinned down at her, leaning in for a kiss, when he suddenly jolted back, frowning. "Don't change the subject! You have to go after what's yours! You cannot just lay down and cede all of your power to someone who doesn't deserve it! Someone who has only hurt you and—"

"Okay."

"—will only continue to take advantage of... what?"

"Okay. I'll do it. After the new year, I'll find a lawyer to help me get what Apollo Tech owes me."

They regarded each other quietly for a moment, each coming to an understanding about the other. Autumn recognized that Irdu needed her to seek justice that he could not seek for himself. He knew that she was agreeing to it solely for that reason. None of it needed to be said out loud.

"So." Autumn twirled towards the kitchen. "I did a little more cooking. I thought maybe you could humor me again and eat Christmas dinner with me?"

Irdu followed her, leaning over her shoulder to look at the various pans and dishes spread on the counter. "What's all this?"

"Well, there's still all of yesterday's leftovers. But today I also roasted a small chicken, some broccoli, *and* carrots." She tapped each pan with a dramatic flourish. "Protein! And vitamins!" She was going to smother the chicken with gravy, the broccoli had been liberally coated in garlic butter and grated parmesan, and the carrots were dressed with honey and rosemary. So, not *healthy*, per se. But definitely more nutritious than yesterday's carbohydrate spectacular.

Not that she was forgetting the carbs. She had yesterday's leftovers heated up—mashed potatoes, gravy, biscuits, and the rest of the pumpkin pie waiting for later. "I also made some cut-out cookies." She showed him the tray with a dozen Santa-shaped cookies iced and decorated. "I used to make them with my grandma every year. After she died, I kept making them on my own. Usually I make a lot more, because I'd give some to friends, and bring some into work, but these past two years…" Anger tightened her throat. "Anyway, even if you don't eat any, you can behold their excellence with your eyes."

Irdu picked up one of the Santa cookies, examining the elaborate icing job. "These are works of art."

She grinned. "I know."

"They're beautiful. How does anybody ever eat them?"

"That's what everybody always says. So I usually make a big show of biting Santa's head off." She giggled, remembering the way her friend Liz had screamed the first time she'd seen Autumn do it. "They always get eaten pretty quickly after that."

To Autumn's surprise, Irdu lifted the cookie to his mouth and bit Santa's head clean off. He grinned, fangs smeared with red icing. Autumn laughed brightly and set to making plates for both of them. Again, she only put small samples of everything on Irdu's plate. But tonight, instead of poking at it and only trying little nibbles, he cleared his plate.

"Would you like more?" she asked, trying to sound casual.

"Would you like me to eat more?"

Some of her joy deflated. He wasn't eating more food because he was becoming more human. He was just trying to make her happy. Still, the fact that he cared enough to bother made her feel loved, so she shook her head and helped herself to a second slice of pumpkin pie.

"Do you want to get dressed and go for a walk?" Autumn asked as she ate the last bite of pie. "We can go look at the Christmas lights."

Irdu wiped a smudge of whipped cream from the corner of her mouth and licked it from his thumb. "Let's go."

He was in the process of pulling on his cargo pants when Autumn's phone lit up. She glanced at it, and sighed.

Irdu looked up. "What's wrong?"

"Nothing. I just have to take this call." She brought the phone to her ear. "Hey, Mom. Merry Christmas."

"Merry Christmas, Autumn. How have you been?"

Every year, there was an obligatory Christmas call with her mother in which they both asked stilted questions about each other's lives, wished each other well, and then said goodbye with mutual relief. This year's call went infinitely smoother than last year's, when Autumn realized she had failed to tell her mother that she and Dylan had broken up six months prior.

Regardless of how well the calls with her mother went, they always left Autumn feeling hollowed out. She'd like to give them up entirely. She dreamed of saying, "Listen, you don't care about me. It's obvious. Let's save ourselves both the time and effort, and just stop trying." But you can't say those sorts of things to your mother. So the calls continued.

Irdu, half-dressed, sensed her disquiet and drifted over to her while she listened to her mom talk about her stepdaughter's recent engagement.

"Oh. Wow. That's great. Give Maggie my congratulations, okay?" Her mother had never been able to remember Dylan's name when they were together—calling him Devon, Declan, Damien, Dermot—and while she knew his company had something to do with tech, she never seemed to understand that he made software, not physical computers. In contrast, she knew everything about Maggie's fiancé from his childhood nickname to his favorite color.

"He sounds great," Autumn said, with adequately feigned interest. "Maggie must be so happy with him."

Irdu's big hand landed on the nape of her neck and squeezed gently.

"So..." Her mother paused, and Autumn knew the most painfully awkward part of the conversation was coming. "What are you doing today?"

Last year, filled with bitterness, she'd bluntly told her mother that she was having an orphan's Christmas, since she had nobody else to spend it with. She'd regretted the words immediately. This year, the warmth of Irdu's presence steadied her, and she was able to calmly say, "I'm spending the day with a friend. We just had a big dinner. Now we're going to go see the Christmas lights."

"Oh, good." Her mom sounded genuinely relieved. Last year's bluntness had made an impact, apparently. "You know, you're welcome to spend Christmas with us. We'd love to have you."

No, they wouldn't. The words rang of forced politeness.

"That'd be great. Maybe next year."

"Definitely!" her mom said, too brightly. "Well, I'll let you go enjoy the Christmas lights. Talk to you later."

"Bye, mom."

Autumn set her phone face down and turned away from it. Irdu still had a hand on her shoulder, his eyes full of sympathy. "Do you still want to go for a walk?"

"Yeah."

They got dressed and went out. Irdu kept a comforting arm around Autumn's shoulders as they wandered the streets. A few blocks over, there was a street where all the houses always went all-out with their Christmas displays. The entire street was lit up like daylight—if daylight were a kaleidoscope of colors, blinking and strobing and swirling over every surface. Even behind his sunglasses, Irdu squinted against the brightness.

While Irdu had become somewhat accustomed to mingling with other people, his excitement at being able to do so was still palpable. Autumn smiled and eased against him as he looked around at all the other people who'd come out to see the lights. Children tugged on their parents' hands and shrieked their delight at the displays. Couples walked hand in hand, just as she and Irdu were doing. Up the street, a group of carolers were singing *O Holy Night.*

They stayed out for a long time, strolling in contented silence. Eventually, the cold got to Autumn. When Irdu noticed she was trying to hide her shivering, he insisted on taking her back home.

Back at the apartment, they undressed and got into bed. Holding Irdu, letting his warmth seep into her, Autumn let out a happy sigh. This was not the life she'd expected to be living. But it was somehow better. She twisted around, pushing Irdu onto his back and climbing astride him. He caught her hands, rubbing them between his own.

"You're still cold."

"I'm warming up." She pulled out of his grasp. "Hands behind your head," she said with a wolfish grin. Now that she knew how very much he liked being bossed around, she used it to her advantage. "And keep them there."

He obeyed, his eyes shifting to black as he watched her inch her way down his body. She teased and tortured him with her fingers and mouth until he came. She felt his climax coast over her tongue, sparkling like champagne, hot like cinnamon. A wave of power, rich and deep, washed through her body. Her eyes rolled back in her head, and darkness enveloped her.

The cold hit her immediately.

She stood at the base of the tower this time. Indistinct bodies, sallow and gray, milled around her. When they brushed against her, the cold deepened. It was a relentless burn, eating its way to her very bones. With painful effort, she tilted her head back to survey the tower standing over her. Black stone gleamed, reflecting the fires from the forge. Winged demons circled overhead. Lesser demons, stooped with exhaustion, hauled blocks of stone into place, stacking the walls ever higher.

From the peak of the half-constructed tower, pale white

eyes fixed upon Autumn. She felt the gaze like a physical touch, wrapping her in a constricting hold, squeezing the breath from her lungs. The cold became too painful to bear. She wanted to scream, but her throat was frozen.

Trespasser, a malevolent voice hissed, echoing inside her head. It chased away all other thoughts, swelling against her skull until Autumn thought her head would split open. ***None may enter who do not pay their fare. How will you pay, trespasser?***

Autumn tried to fight, tried to scream, but her body was immobile, her voice gone. Her only defense was to close her eyes, shutting out the sight of those furious, pale, inhuman eyes. She thought of Irdu, willing her way back to him.

A faint thread of warmth splintered through the cold. The grip around her lungs eased. She hauled in a gasping breath.

When she opened her eyes, she was back in her bedroom, back with Irdu, as if no time had passed at all. He was still recovering from his climax, hips rolling beneath her hands, chest heaving with desperate breaths. Autumn opened her mouth, releasing him. When she breathed out, curling blue fog rose from her parted lips.

The cold burn dissipated from beneath her skin, warmth from Irdu's body chasing through her. When he lifted his head, the black was fading from his eyes, revealing electric blue irises. But then the unusual blue faded too, revealing brown irises and round, human pupils. The blue leached from his skin, the cuneiform tattoos flickering and vanishing, until he had brown skin and black hair. His fangs and claws receded, leaving flat human teeth and fingernails. His horns vanished.

Autumn stared at him. It wasn't the first time she'd seen him like this, but it was the first time she'd seen the change happen. And it seemed to be... sticking.

Food! she remembered. In many of the katabasis myths, the

heroes were revived by food and water. She leapt from the bed, filled a glass of water and grabbed a slice of roast chicken.

"Here!" she pressed the glass into his hand, sloshing it on the bed. "Drink!"

He gave her a perplexed look. But when he lifted the glass to his mouth, he caught sight of his hand and dropped the glass in shock. Water spilled everywhere. He stared at his hands, mouth agape.

"Autumn!"

"I know! Here!" She thrust the chicken at him. "Eat!"

"What? Why?"

"Just do it!"

He chewed the chicken and swallowed it, looking shell-shocked the entire time. Autumn ran to the sink and refilled the glass of water. This time he managed not to drop it, and drank it all down.

"I don't know what's happening. This isn't a dream state. Is it? Have you put *me* into a dream state?"

"I don't know how to do that."

"You'd figure it out."

"This is real, Irdu. I don't know precisely how. But it's not the first time. This morning, you were human when I woke up. And you stayed here for a few minutes past sunrise. And you looked human for a split-second last night."

"Then it's not permanent."

"No, but it's getting stronger—lasting longer. I've been doing some research into Underworld mythology, and I've come across—"

"What? Why didn't you tell me?"

"Because I knew it would upset you. You kept asking if I was going to kill myself before." She waved away his consternation. "Anyways, in a lot of stories, people who leave the underworld are revived by eating food. So, I've been feeding you."

Irdu glowered at her.

"You said it wouldn't kill you."

"You should have told me you were running experiments on me."

"I didn't want to get your hopes up."

Irdu looked back down at his hands. He whisked the blanket away to look at the rest of his body. He ran his hands along his spine, feeling the smooth place where his tail used to be. He slid his fingers through his hair, rubbing at the spots where his horns normally emerged.

"I don't know what this means," he said shakily.

"It means we can get you out!"

He shook his head in disbelief.

"Seriously, think about it. You told me there's a ritual for bringing a soul to the Underworld, right? A demon feeds you, marks you, and calls you by your full name?"

"Something like that," Irdu muttered evasively.

"Well, I've fed you. I've marked you. And I know your real name. But instead of taking you to the Underworld, I'm bringing you here."

"It can't work," Irdu said. "The soul exchange is just that— an *exchange*. Nothing's being exchanged here. Nobody is taking my place." Sudden alarm crossed his face. He surged forward, catching Autumn's face between his hands. "You're still human?" He peered into her eyes, pulled her lip down to examine her teeth, ran his fingers through her hair, feeling for horns.

"Yes!" She bit at his fingers when he tried to check her teeth again. She got out of bed and started fixing a big plate. "You need to eat while you're human. As much as you can. I think it's the key to keeping you here."

Still looking completely freaked out, Irdu nonetheless accepted the plate she shoved into his hands and began eating.

"Does it feel any different from when you eat in your demon form?"

He swiped a slice of roast chicken through mashed potatoes and gravy and shoved it into his mouth. "Yes," he said through the mouthful. He chewed and swallowed. "It's... nice. It tastes good." He ate more. And more. He ate until the crammed plate was emptied.

"Do you want pie?"

"Yes."

Grinning, Autumn loaded a slice with whipped cream and gave it to him. He ignored the fork she brought and picked it up in one hand, taking giant bites.

"Good?" Autumn asked.

He nodded enthusiastically.

"Help yourself to more. I'll be right back." She went to the bathroom and shut the door. Leaning over the sink, she tilted her head to examine the spot beneath her jaw that was still burning with cold.

She could make out a faint purple shadow beneath her skin, just over her pulse point. She could almost let herself believe it was a bruise. But the shape was too finely angular, composed of interconnecting lines. It was cuneiform. As she stared at it, cold dread washed over her. She recognized that symbol. She'd drawn it from Irdu's body, and had it translated by Leila Kader.

Slave.

She dug in her drawer for concealer and applied it liberally to the mark. When she emerged from the bathroom, Irdu was standing at the stove, still human, picking bits of chicken off the bones. She pulled a hoodie out of her dresser and slid into it, fluffing the hood up around her neck. She knew the mark was unequivocally a *very bad thing*, but if she told Irdu about it, he'd do something too drastic, like blame himself for it and then let himself dissipate.

So, okay. Trying to bring Irdu back to the mortal realm was not the simple maneuver she'd thought it would be. She should have known. In the stories, there's always a price for leaving. For Inanna, two different deities had to take her place in order for her to leave the Underworld. For Osiris, even after being resurrected by Isis, he had to return to the Underworld as the resident deity. For Persephone, leaving was only a temporary respite, from which she would be recalled again and again throughout eternity.

Autumn's heart began to race. *Nothing's set in stone,* she tried to soothe herself. *You're still human. You just have one little mark. Irdu's humanness fades, your mark will probably fade too. You have to stop* trying *to see the Underworld when you come.*

She glanced over at Irdu, who had sandwiched broccoli, pumpkin pie, and chicken in a buttered biscuit and was dunking it in gravy. She couldn't ask him to stop eating—to stop *trying* to be human. But what if the only alternative was to give up her own humanity?

Irdu took a bite of his layered biscuit monstrosity. He chewed, then grimaced at the taste. After a moment's hesitation, he kept chewing.

She repressed a smile.

Tomorrow. She'd figure it out tomorrow.

Irdu caught sight of her. He gave a hard swallow, clearing his mouth, then smiled rakishly at her. There was broccoli caught between several of his teeth. "Well, hello there, gorgeous. How about a tumble with a real, live, *human* man?" He waggled his brows.

"Being human has given you an appetite for more than just food, I see."

He rounded the counter and caught her in his arms. "I want you no matter what form I take." He tossed her on the bed and leapt after her. He crawled up her body, bracing himself over her. "But I want to know—to *really* know—what's it's like to be with you as a normal man." He peeled her sweater off and stripped her pants away.

She wanted to give him every possible pleasure he could experience in his human body. She touched every inch of him—running her fingers through his hair without the impediment of horns, stroking the length of his spine without having a tail to grip at the end, sucking his blunt fingertips into her mouth, stroking her tongue across his full bottom lip without feeling the press of fangs. She wrapped her legs around his waist, aware of the absence of his tail curling around her leg or stroking her flank. She looked into his eyes—brown, human eyes that glazed with pleasure, but otherwise remained unchanged.

When they came, there was no enveloping darkness, no glittering blue haze. There was only each other, holding on, riding their shared pleasure. They lay together, glowing with warmth, sated and peaceful.

Irdu stroked her hair. He watched his brown-skinned hand as it slid through her dark locks. "I wonder how much longer I have before I change back."

"Maybe all night. When I woke up yesterday morning, you were like this. I'm not sure how long it lasted." She froze, suddenly alarmed. "What happens if you get called back to the Underworld and you haven't harvested an orgasm in your demon form?"

Irdu blinked. "I don't know." He suddenly pulled her close. She felt his cock harden against her belly. "Can you take me again?" he asked.

"Yes."

He turned her onto her stomach and pulled her hips up. His hands sank into the mattress on either side of her shoulders, and his chest pressed against her back. She felt the blunt tip of him nudge against her folds, and then he was inside her again. She thrust back against him, savoring the feeling of being completely enclosed by his body.

She came before him, arching up against the weight of his body, shuddering and crying as the potent pleasure of orgasm combined with the awareness of his closeness, the feel of his body still with her. It hurt to be given something so perfect, and know it had to be taken away. A tear slipped down her cheek, and then another.

When he came, he gripped her arms hard, his face pressed to her shoulder as he gritted his teeth and groaned through the pleasure. As the last wave of his climax shuddered through him, he withdrew from her, and gathered her into his arms.

They lay together in the silence, listening to their breaths, feeling the beat of their hearts. A gentle touch turned into a searching caress. A tender touch of lips turned into a deep, hard kiss. They melded together again and again that night. They had each other in every conceivable way. As the night shifted closer to dawn, and Irdu remained in his human form, the possible finality of their situation weighed over them both.

"I love you," Autumn whispered hoarsely.

Irdu's face was stark with emotion as he gazed back at her.

"I do. I just need you to know that." She buried her face against his chest so he wouldn't see her tears, but he felt them.

"Don't cry, Autumn." He tilted her chin up, kissed away her tears.

"It's not fair. None of this is fair."

"*Shhh*. Nothing's written in stone."

She shook her head. She needed to tell him the truth, tell him about the mark on her neck. She couldn't form the words. She'd no doubt sweated away the concealer she'd put over it, but it was small and placed in a shadowed part of her neck. It would be easy to miss. She reached for her neck, ready to point out the mark to him.

But before her eyes, Irdu began to shift. It started with his skin. The warm golden-brown bleached away, turning cooler and cooler, until finally it bled into blue. The cuneiform tattoos snaked their way across his body. His horns and claws curled outward. His tail announced itself with a flick.

"You—you changed back!" She grabbed her phone to check the time. There was only an hour until sunrise. "Quick! We have to—" She clutched his face and kissed him frantically.

Irdu caught her wrists, pulling her hands away, and pinned them above her head. "It's alright, love. We've got time." He kissed her, keeping her wrists pinned. It was a gentle, sweet kiss. She arched up, trying to deepen it, but he pulled back, keeping it soft and light.

"Irdu!" she twisted in his hold. "This is important!"

"I know." His other hand caught her hip, pinning her flat to the mattress. He feathered light kisses along her jaw and her throat.

She whined her frustration.

His lips came back to her mouth, soft and easy. He kissed her like that for long minutes, until the tension eased from her body. The hand on her hip slid between her thighs, cupping her sex. He rubbed gently, a steady pressure, and kept kissing her. Slowly, almost imperceptibly, everything about his touches and kisses became a little harder, a little faster. It grew and grew, until Autumn was gasping into his mouth, her hips rocking to meet the tease of his fingers. At last, she shattered apart.

When she came back to herself, instead of watching the blue haze clear from Irdu's eyes, he was staring at her in abject horror.

"Are you okay?" she asked, sitting up. "What's wrong?" She reached for his face, and when she saw her own skin, she froze.

Faint purple cuneiform marks were spidering across her arms, becoming more and more clear. She looked down at her body and found more of the same. Frantic, she felt her teeth, her hair —but there were no fangs and no horns. Her fingernails were ordinary, rounded human nails.

The cuneiform continued to darken, becoming more and more clear against the neutral tone of her skin. She looked back up at Irdu, unable to hide the fear in her eyes. "What's happening?" she whispered.

The horror had faded from Irdu's face, leaving a mask of such inconsolable grief that Autumn began to cry. Fat tears rolled down her cheeks as she stared at him.

"This is what I feared," he said hoarsely. "You've managed to trigger the soul exchange ritual. I didn't—" His voice broke. He took a ragged breath. "I didn't think it could be initiated by the victim." He pushed away from her, scrambling off the bed.

"Irdu—"

"*Never* say my name again! You'll damn yourself."

"But, listen—"

"I shouldn't have taken food from you. I should have known it would be a risk." His face twisted into a self-loathing grimace. "But the marks? You haven't marked me..."

"I bit you," she said, a defeated whisper.

"That's not enough. It has to be—" his gaze fell on the narrow shelf where she stored her art supplies. "You painted me," he said darkly.

"So?"

"It's the perfect inverse. Instead of *me* putting my mark *on* you, you've made me *into* a mark. You've created a graven image of me."

"I'm not worshipping it!"

"No." He looked back at her, eyes bleak. "But love is a kind of worship."

"I can't stop loving you!"

"You must." He grabbed the canvas of his portrait off the top of her dresser and broke it over his knee. Autumn cried out in shock. He ripped the canvas from the frame, using his claws to slice it into a thousand shreds.

"Stop!"

He spun back to her art supplies and pulled out her sketch book.

"What are you doing?"

He flipped through the pages until he found the drawing of him. He ripped it out of the sketchbook.

"No, stop!"

He tore the page in half.

Autumn scrambled off the bed. "Irdu!"

"*Never say my name again!*" he snarled so viciously, it made her draw up short. His expression faltered at the fear in her eyes, rage giving way to sorrow again. Outside her bedroom window, the sky was beginning to lighten. "I'm sorry. It has to be this way." He began tearing the drawing into hundreds of pieces. "You must burn both of these when I'm gone."

There was a finality to his words that terrified her. "When you're gone?"

"I'm not coming back to you tonight, Autumn."

Her throat burned. Tears flooded her eyes until she couldn't see. "*No...*"

"I'll let myself dissipate, as I should have done millennia ago."

"Please, no! Don't do this—we can figure something out!"

"We can't. The cards have always been stacked against us." He let out a bitter laugh. "How many times do I have to learn this lesson?"

Autumn managed to stumble to him. She threw her arms

around him, holding for dear life. "Please don't do this. Please, please stay with me! You can't die."

"I've been dead for more than four thousand years." His arms came around her, and he pulled her tightly against him. "Being with you has been a privilege I had no right to." He cupped her face and tilted her head back. He pressed a gentle kiss to her tear-soaked cheek. "I love you. I don't deserve to, but I love you. I want you to have a good life, and I'm a threat to that. When you remember me, always know that I left you because I loved you."

"*Please—*"

The first gleam of sunlight edged over the city's rooftops. The light shone through her window, limning his face with gold. The markings on Autumn's skin pulsed, then vanished.

Irdu pressed a kiss to the top of her head. "Goodbye, Autumn. I love you."

And then he was gone.

Chapter Eleven

Autumn stood in the wreckage of her apartment, numb.

The entire world was silent, and she stood in the very center of it—the smoking shell at the epicenter of a bomb blast.

A thousand years passed. A million.

Or maybe only minutes. But when Autumn finally managed to move again, her body felt like a withered husk. She looked down at the shredded remains of her art. She fell to her knees and scooped them up in her hands. Confetti. His strong hands and sharp claws had turned everything practically to pulp. She let the scraps sift through her fingers and flutter back to the floor.

Her sketchbook lay open on the ground where Irdu had dropped it. The next page after her drawing of him was still intact—his tattoos. She picked the sketchbook up and stared at the tattoos.

Night. Body. Slave.

Brutalized by the greed of others, punished for trying to take back his own life. Now condemned to die again.

A scream welled in her throat.

Useless. Useless to scream. Useless to cry. Useless to beg, to bargain, or to plea.

But there was something she could do.

She could *descend*.

Chapter Twelve

Since her teens, Autumn had been able to control her dreams. It sometimes took her a little while to realize she was dreaming. But once she did, she could push the dream in any direction. Lots of people could do it—there was even a name for it: lucid dreaming. When she was young, she thought of it as telling herself a story—an immersive fiction that she could manipulate.

But as she grew older, she began to understand that dreams weren't separate from reality. The happiness, fear, hope, and sorrow that she felt in her dreams lingered into the waking world. The worries and obsessions of the waking world chased her into her dreams. In dreams, she'd worked through the grief of her father's death, because her waking mind couldn't process it. And it was in dreams, too, that she'd come to accept that her relationship with her mother was irrevocably broken. When she dreamt, she created art for her hands to translate when she was awake. She'd dreamt the website design that had saved Dylan's company.

Dreams weren't the antithesis of reality—they were an extension of it.

It was through dreams that she had met Irdu. And it was through dreams that she would find him again.

Autumn stripped herself naked and tied up her hair. She took the sketchbook page with Irdu's tattoos and began redrawing him from memory. But when she drew in his tattoos, she made a few, tiny adjustments. When she was done, she took a permanent marker and covered her body in the same tattoos, repeating their meanings in her mind as she wrote. *Dream. Body. Death. Descend. Bridge. Power. Return.*

When all of her skin was covered, she dropped the drawing, letting it fall to the floor. She crawled into bed and waited for the exhaustion of the previous night to take her under.

She stood on a wide, empty plain. The air was silent and unmoving. A wall, unfathomably tall, stretched across the infinite width, going on to the ends of the horizon. Directly in front of Autumn, a twisted black gate was set into the wall, in front of which stood a robed figure, easily twenty feet tall. The figure shifted. Its hooded head turned towards Autumn. It clutched a bone stylus in one emaciated hand, and a clay tablet in the other.

You have not yet been called to this realm, mortal. *The voice boomed inside her head like thunder. It did not speak in language, and yet its meaning was crystal clear.* **Turn back.**

She spread her arms, displaying her nakedness. Even her hair was bound up, revealing every inch of the cuneiform written on her skin. "I haven't come to stay," she said in a shaking voice. "I'm here to negotiate."

The massive creature bent low to examine her. Autumn fought the urge to run away.

You bear a claim mark. *The figure's hooded head tilted curiously.* **But you are the claimant.**

"Yes. And I'm here to take what's mine."

The Gatekeeper straightened. **What is taken must be paid.**

"I know."

Then enter, mortal. But understand that the gates of the underworld open only in one direction.

"I understand."

The gates creaked open, revealing at first only darkness. But as Autumn crossed the threshold, the same dark realm she'd seen in her dreams resolved before her eyes. In the distance, the terrible black tower stood. The sides of it glowed orange, reflecting the fire of the forges. Deep fissures scored the ground, radiating out from the tower's base. Lightning split the pitch-black sky, illuminating the figures of winged demons. And ensconced deeply inside the growing tower, a cold presence that Autumn could feel, all the way across the dead-packed plains.

Eyes, so far away, and yet so forcefully present, watched her from within the tower. She felt their regard like needles over her skin. Curious malevolence rolled over her in sickening waves. The cuneiform she'd drawn upon her skin began to burn. Smoke curled from her skin. She hissed at the pain, but would not yield. She tore her gaze away from the malevolent eyes and began her journey to the tower.

Out on the plains, still so far from her destination, she was surrounded by gray, insubstantial bodies. They milled listlessly towards the tower, compelled by some unspoken mission. Their hollow eyes swiveled to fix upon Autumn. Amidst the incorporeal gray, she stood out like a beacon. Vitality glowed from her skin, warm and steady.

She moved forward, and they parted for her. She walked faster, and the dead swept themselves out of her way. They watched her pass with something like reverence in their slack faces.

Their mouths moved in speech, but the words were lost—nothing more than the voiceless rasp of fallen leaves.

The distance to the tower was immeasurable. She felt as if she walked forever. The dead stretched as far as the eye could see. The tower never seemed to grow closer, but the looming glare of that malevolent presence grew stronger and stronger.

And then, without comprehending quite when and how it had happened, Autumn stood at the base of the tower, blinking against the fire-bright flare of the forges. Within them, demons seized the dead and thrust them into the fire, hammering the burning souls into diamond-hard bricks.

Initially blinded by the flames, it took Autumn some time to realize that the fuel for the forges was more bodies. Demons, sprawled on the ground, consumed by flame. The demons were conscious, twitching and writhing in agony. But stakes driven through their hands and feet kept them pinned in place, helpless to escape the roaring fire that licked along their flesh. Their mouths were stretched wide, but their screams were drowned out by the roar of the fire and the noise of the bricks being hammered into shape.

The dead were everywhere. Piling helplessly into the demon-fueled forges, where they were hammered into shape and hoisted up the scaffolding surrounding the tower. The work was continuous and all-consuming. Everywhere she looked, the demons sacrificed the dead for the tower.

The cold white eyes gazed down from the tower's unfinished peak, seeming to bore into Autumn. The symbols she'd drawn on her skin burned anew. She turned away from that hateful gaze, and picked her way around the dead, walking the length of the forges. Something compelled her onward. She didn't know what she was seeking.

Until she found him. *Irdu lay spread-eagle, pinned to the hard rock by spikes driven through his hands and feet. Flame* engulfed his body. His face was a rictus mask of pain. Another demon approached him with a dead soul to be forged into a tower brick. Without thinking, Autumn shoved them aside. Touching them sent bitter cold leaching through her body. She fell to her knees beside Irdu. The fire roiled high overhead, but Autumn couldn't feel the heat.

She reached into the flame and did not burn. The cuneiform on her body lit up with a golden glow. She laid her hand on Irdu's chest. The glow of her markings flowed into him, illuminating his own tattoos. He cried out and opened his eyes. The flames slowly receded until they died away to nothing, leaving cracked, smoking rock beneath Irdu's shuddering body.

When he saw Autumn, his eyes went wide. "No—NO! What have you done? Get out of here!"

She ignored him, reaching for the stake in his nearest hand. She tugged and tugged. Her markings lit golden-bright again, and the stake came free.

"Autumn—stop this! Leave! Now!"

With the same struggle, the same glow, she freed one foot, then the other. At last, she freed his other hand. He jumped up and grabbed her, frenzied.

"You have to leave. You can't let her see you! Please, please, get out of here!"

"The watcher in the tower?" Autumn asked. "She saw me the moment I entered the Underworld. She's watched me this whole time."

Irdu's grip tightened on her shoulders. "What are you doing here?"

"I couldn't let you die."

"I'm already dead. You must leave."

"Not without you."

"There is no other way."

Autumn dug her feet in, refusing to be dragged anywhere. "I have a plan. Is there a scribe? We need to find her."

Shock crossed Irdu's face. "What do you know about the Scribe?"

"Bring me to her."

Irdu sagged. "You've already met the Scribe at the Gates. The only authority on this side of the wall is the Host."

"Then I will have to face the Host."

"No!" Irdu grabbed for her, but she slipped from his grasp and turned to the base of the tower. "You cannot enter the tower," he told her frantically. "There is no way inside except to be called by the Host."

In front of her, the wall melted away, revealing a single door. Inside the door, a staircase spiraled up and out of sight. She had been called.

Autumn stepped onto the first riser. Irdu attempted to come after her, but he crashed against the open doorway as if he'd hit a solid wall. He tried again, and failed again.

"Autumn, please! Don't do this!" Irdu begged.

She turned back and reached across the threshold to cup his face. "I have to." He tried to grab her wrist, to pull her out, but she slipped from his grasp, and turned back to the stairs.

"Autumn! No!"

She began the climb.

She could feel the watcher—the Host—anticipating her. That cold malevolence grew thicker, more brutal, with each step. Just as when she'd crossed the plains, she seemed to climb forever under the cold watch of the Host—and then, very suddenly, she reached a landing.

She was at the top of the tower. There was no ceiling. Over the edges of the incomplete walls, she could see to every horizon. It was nothing but lightless emptiness, filled with the souls of the dead, waiting to be smelted into the Host's tower.

Welcome, Trespasser. Have you come to pay your fare? *The Host had taken the form of a woman. But not just any woman. She wore the face of Autumn's mother. It was a face not unlike Autumn's own—round-cheeked, with thick dark brows and a pointed chin—except for the eyes, which were an empty, crystalline white. Incomprehensible power radiated from her with nearly physical force. Autumn had to strain to remain in the room.*

"I've come to make a bargain."

The Host smiled. **You are in no position to do such a thing.**

"I am, actually. I've put a claim on a demon."

By doing so, you bind yourself to us. *The Host waved her hand, and a select portion of the symbols drawn on Autumn's body lit up—only one specific symbol, everywhere that she'd written it on herself.* Death. *Over and over again—on her throat, over her heart, on her hands, her legs, her feet.* Death, death, death.

"You did not look closely enough," Autumn told her. Each and every death *symbol on her body was sandwiched between two others—the character for* language *and the character for* power. *Autumn reached into her bound hair and pulled the marker from where she'd tucked it before she'd gone to sleep. Starting on her left hand, she added a fourth symbol:* love.

The Host smirked. **Human emotions have no power here.** *Her face shifted, and instead of looking at her mother, Autumn found herself facing Dylun. His handsome face stared at her with the Host's blazing eyes.*

"Were you human once?" Autumn asked, continuing to add love *all over her body.*

We have been many things.

"Are you even conscious? Or are you acting on instinct?" She

nearly had every language-death-power *modified with an added* love. *The Host watched with undisguised interest.*

We are aware of ourself.

"What did the dead do before you began building your tower?"

The Host's face shifted from Dylan's to her father's. That one gave Autumn pause. She swallowed hard, looked back down at her legs, and continued writing.

They were purified in the fire and released.

"Reincarnation?"

The Host shrugged. **It is a place and a time we have not experienced.**

"So why do you keep them here, now? Why are you trapping them in this tower?"

We build the tower to the edge of the Underworld. We build the tower to escape Death.

"You are *death."*

The Host's face shifted from her father's to her grandmother's. **Death is final. We seek eternity.**

"You could have it. You could cleanse yourself in the fire and be released. You could allow the dead to be released, instead of condemning them to eternity in servitude."

The unknown is not eternity. It is oblivion. It is the end.

"What right do you have to steal that end from the dead?"

We have the right, because we have taken it. *The Host's face shifted to Irdu's.*

Autumn flinched. "So you can't be persuaded?"

The Host laughed. It was an inhuman sound, lacking any real emotion. **You do not have the power to compel us.**

Autumn drew the last love *over her heart. The strain of staying in the tower suddenly vanished. She stood straighter, facing the Host head-on. "If you can't be compelled, then you must be destroyed."*

The Host's face faded back to her own—the one Autumn had first seen. An indistinct face, as hollow as that of the dead. **You do not have the power to destroy us.**

Autumn gave her a sympathetic look. "You have destroyed yourself." She walked to the wall, braced her hands against it, and pushed. Bricks dislodged, tumbling away. Autumn peered over the edge, watching them fall. They hit the ground and shattered into dust. As if caught in a tiny whirlwind, the dust twisted and spun, reforming into the bodies of the dead.

STOP THIS.

Autumn braced her hands against the wall. The markings on her skin glowed brightly. She pushed again and more bricks tumbled. She kept pushing and pushing, dismantling the entire wall.

ENOUGH. *The Host reached for her, but her hand passed through as if Autumn were made of smoke.*

"You did this to yourself," Autumn said. She lifted her foot and brought her heel to the floor with a powerful stomp. The bricks fell away beneath her feet. She and the Host both tumbled down. Autumn landed on her hands and knees, surrounded by debris. She launched herself upright and threw herself into dismantling the tower. The Host thundered and raged, but she couldn't stop Autumn. Her voice grew weaker with each collapsing wall, each demolished floor.

One by one, the forges blinked out as the tower tumbled down, faster and faster. Story after story gave way beneath Autumn's relentless drive. She heard the sound of voices, and footsteps. A flood of demons poured into the tower—Irdu at their lead. They surrounded Autumn, joined her in the destruction.

Eons seemed to pass. She stood shoulder to shoulder with Irdu, pulling the tower apart brick by brick. The demons who had once circled the tower on wing now clung to the sides, ripping at the walls.

When they reached the lowest floor, the Host was a diminished thing, sagging against the wall, looking no more substantial than any of the other dead. Her mouth worked again and again, trying to issue the same command, but no sound emerged. Feeling no pity, Autumn and Irdu pushed down the final wall. The bricks fell away in a collapsing wave, shattering to dust, and then reforming into the dead.

The Host became more and more indistinct, her features ever-shifting and blurred. As Autumn kicked the very last brick away, the Host shattered into dust. The dust sifted and swirled, reforming into six different dead souls. They looked around in bleak confusion. When they saw each other, they surged together, but try as they might, they could not reform into the Host.

A soft wind stirred the air, and every dead soul in the Underworld lifted their faces to it. The hollowness receded from their eyes. The wind grew a little stronger. The spot where the tower had once stood began to glow, as golden bright as the markings on Autumn's skin.

One of the dead stepped into it. She lifted her face with a soft smile, and when she opened her mouth a gentle laugh emerged. She dissolved away into the golden light, but her laugh remained, echoing through the silence of the Underworld like the ringing of a bell.

Autumn found Irdu's hand and clutched it. They watched as another one of the dead stepped into the light, and with a smile and sigh of relief, he too, dissolved into light. More and more of the dead stepped into the glowing circle, dissipating with looks of joy on their faces.

Autumn twisted, looking up at Irdu. He met her gaze and they moved in sync—she leapt on him, wrapping her legs around his waist as he hauled her up against his body.

"What have you done?" he demanded between gasping kisses. "You insane... reckless... genius..."

"Saved you." She clung to him. Tears burned her eyes. "I had to save you. Tell me you'll be alright now. Tell me you won't dissipate." A glow enveloped them, glittering and blue.

"I don't know if I'll—"

She couldn't feel his hands on her anymore. "Irdu? What's happening?"

"Autumn?" His voice sounded far away. The light grew brighter, blinding her.

"Irdu!"

"Autumn!"

The light faded, and she found herself standing outside the gates of the Underworld again. The Gatekeeper loomed over her.

Your claim has been forfeit, mortal. You have no right to the Underworld.

"What does that mean? I no longer have a claim on Irdu? What's happened to him?"

The living are not privy to the affairs of the dead.

"Dead?" she choked on the word, doubling over on a shock of pain. "It can't be. He's immortal. He's a demon!"

The living are not privy to affairs of the dead, *the Gatekeeper echoed.*

"No! Tell me what's happened to Irdu! I demand—"

The Gatekeeper waved a cloaked hand. **Return to your domain.**

AUTUMN WOKE WITH A SCREAM. OUTSIDE HER bedroom window, the sky was dark. She'd slept through the entire day. She sat upright in an empty bed.

She was alone.

Chapter Thirteen

Autumn collapsed back onto her bed with a choked sob. She'd failed. Her vision blurred and she squeezed her eyes shut as hot tears slicked her cheeks. She curled in on herself, wracked with silent sobs that robbed her of breath and made her chest ache as if her heart had been ripped out. Or maybe her chest ached *because* her heart had been ripped out.

A low noise echoed through her room. Autumn froze. It had sounded a lot like a male groan. Sitting up cautiously, she peered over the edge of her bed.

Sprawled on the floor where she'd left the drawing of Irdu lay a naked man—a naked man with warm brown skin and black hair. Faint markings traced over his body, almost indistinguishable from the rest of his skin, like well-healed scars. A very distinct scar carved a thick, ragged line across his throat. Piercings that had once been golden bright were now a dull, tarnished gray. He had a muscular arm thrown over his face, but he groaned and turned, letting his arm fall away. He had a face Autumn had once thought of as brutish and unhandsome. But time had improved her vision, and she now saw a face that was harshly beautiful. Beautiful—and *human*.

Unable to make a noise through a throat choked with emotion, Autumn flopped onto the floor and crawled over to Irdu's sprawled body. She touched him gently, afraid that her hand would go through him and he would vanish like smoke. But when she laid her palm on his chest, his body was solid, and warm, and real.

His eyes fluttered open, and he stared up at her, dazed.

"Irdu?" she whispered hoarsely.

The dazedness faded, and his eyes warmed. "Autumn?"

"Are you alright?" She was crying again, her tears spattering his chest.

"I... think so?" He reached up, cupped her cheek. "How'd you do it?"

The gatekeeper's words echoed in her mind. **The living are not privy to the affairs of the dead.** She'd forfeit her claim on Irdu—and therefore her access to the Underworld— not because he was dead, but because he was *living*.

She touched the faint scars of his tattoos. "I changed their meaning. I made a new image of you. But I changed your tattoos in the image. I took away the gods' marks. I rewrote the character *slave* as *man*. And I changed the *death* character to *love*."

Irdu pushed himself up slowly, grimacing. Autumn caught his arm, helping him. "How did you know to do that?"

"The tower in Borsippa—the one where you... died..."

He nodded.

"It was built for a god of literacy, Nabu. You had his mark on your body."

He frowned. "The priests... as I was dying..."

"You also had Inanna's mark—a fertility goddess who had descended into the Underworld. And I thought, maybe, the language was key. You were covered in references to sex, death, and slavery. I realized they were probably what had condemned you to be an incubus. I thought if only your tattoos could be changed, then maybe your fate could be changed. And then I realized, after you got so upset that I had created a 'graven image' of you, that I *did* have the power to change your tattoos."

Irdu stared at her in wonder.

"I knew about the tower in the Underworld. I kept seeing it when we had sex."

He frowned. "You should have told me—"

"You would've decided to end yourself even sooner." She wasn't going to apologize for keeping him from martyring himself. "Anyways, I could tell the tower was bad. I knew there was something inside it, something corrupt. Whatever it was, it held the key to your freedom. Your enslavement was tied to it. Because it held the key to death itself."

"The Host."

She nodded. "And I thought, if I can fight that thing, I can free him."

Irdu shook his head in disbelief. "How did you know you could destroy the Host?"

"Because I love you. I covered myself in my love for you." She held up her arms, showing the imitations of his tattoos inked all over her skin. "I had to hide it until I was inside the tower, so that she would think I was harmless and let me in. But once I was there, the Host's corruption couldn't withstand real love."

"How did I ever doubt you?" he asked. "I never will again. If you tell me you can flap your arms and fly to the moon, I'll believe you." His expression turned fervent. "I owe *everything* to you."

"No. You saved me, too. I was drowning in loneliness. Every

day was getting harder and harder to keep going. If you hadn't come along..." She trailed off into fraught silence.

Irdu gently touched her cheek, bringing her gaze back to him. "I love you, Autumn. I love you more than life."

"Love me enough to *stay* alive. No more noble attempts at self-sacrifice, okay? Because I love you, too. And if I had to live without you—"

Irdu threw his arms around her and hauled her against his body, crushing the words out of her. She held him just as fiercely. They remained like that for a long time.

Eventually, Autumn drew back. She kissed him softly and looked into his dark brown eyes. "I happen to remember that the last time you were in human form you were ravenously hungry and also quite..."

"Horny?"

She traced her finger along his hairline. No horns. "Yes. That's the one. I was just wondering if—" she shrieked as he suddenly flipped her onto the floor. He pounced over her, grinning a fangless smile.

"Are you offering to see to my needs?"

"I was hoping you'd see to mine."

And he did. Several times that night. When she came, she saw only Irdu, felt only pleasure and love. When they weren't attached to each other's bodies, they gorged on Christmas leftovers. Sated and exhausted, they fell asleep in each other's arms.

When she woke in the morning, Irdu was still there. Unconscious and drooling on the pillow, but *there*. And human. Golden sunlight poured through the window, highlighting his features with a sharp-edged glow. Autumn traced a wondering finger over the harsh lines of his face, waiting.

But the sunlight only grew brighter, and Irdu stayed with her.

Epilogue

"So he was raised in a *cult?*" Liz reiterated for the hundredth time. The two of them were standing in Liz's kitchen, waiting for coffee to brew.

"Yep." Autumn accepted a cup of coffee from Liz, and glanced over her shoulder towards the living room, where Irdu sat with Liz's husband, Marcus. The two men were hunched over Marcus's cell phone, exclaiming over a video clip of a newly hatched iguana escaping dozens of hungry snakes.

"So he was just this stateless mystery man—"

"He's not stateless. He's American," Autumn interrupted quickly. It was technically true. Now.

"Okay, but he didn't have a social security number or a birth certificate—"

"He's got a social security number now. He's a real person!"

"I just don't understand how he managed to *live*. How'd he get a job without a social security number? How'd he travel anywhere without ID?"

"The cult was self-sustaining. They had a farm." Autumn hated lying, but how else was she supposed to explain Irdu's past? She usually tried to move the conversation away from that topic as quickly as possible, but Liz was a journalist, and when she smelled a story, she was as tenacious as a bloodhound.

"He seems way too aware of the world for somebody raised by an isolated cult."

"It wasn't like one of those fundamentalist compounds. He interacted with the outside world. They even had a television."

"This sounds like a very permissive cult," Liz said skeptically.

Autumn shrugged and pulled up her default conversation-killer. "He really doesn't like to talk about it, and it's not my place to say anything."

Liz pursed her lips, giving Autumn a narrow-eyed look.

"Don't do your Lois Lane thing on me. This is his personal life, not breaking news."

Liz leaned back, raising her hands in surrender. "You're right. Sorry."

They gathered up coffee cups and brought them into the living room. Autumn handed one to Irdu and sank down on the couch next to him. Irdu looked up, giving her a silent thanks.

"So, Irdu," Liz said. "I hear congratulations are in order."

Irdu looked at Autumn. "Ah, yes. Apollo Tech settled their case with Autumn. Her lawyer negotiated a significant—"

Liz turned to Autumn, appalled. "You didn't tell me!"

"It's all kind of embarrassing." She looked down at her coffee. "I let him take advantage of me, and I was too cowardly to do anything about it until Irdu badgered me into it."

"You're not a coward." Irdu put an arm around her. "You're overly empathetic."

"There's no doubt about that," Liz said. "But I was talking about you, Irdu. Autumn said you passed your GED test?"

"He got a 790. That puts him in the ninety-ninth percentile," Autumn boasted. Irdu gave her a bemused look.

"Yes, I did." he said to Liz. "Thank you."

"So, what's next, then? Career-wise?" Liz asked, with all the intensity of a father cross-examining his daughter's prom date.

"*Liz,*" Autumn objected.

Irdu wasn't bothered. "I've applied to several local universities. I'd like to study history. I'm enjoying my work at the library, but I think I'd like to teach."

"*Oooh*, teaching." Liz shuddered. "So many children."

"Irdu likes being around people," Autumn said fondly. "I think he'd love to be in a classroom every day. And he'd make a really good teacher."

Liz's gaze flicked between the two of them. The tension dissolved from her posture, and she gave Irdu a warm smile.

"I'm sure he would be."

"Speaking of jobs," Autumn said. "I accepted an offer from the Art Institute."

Liz's eyes flew wide. "Autumn!" she shrieked, almost directly in Matthew's ear. He winced. "Sorry, babe." Liz patted the side of his head absently while she glared at Autumn. "You good-news-withholding bitch! Why didn't you tell me right away?"

～

"I'M SORRY ABOUT LIZ. SHE CAN BE KIND OF INTENSE. But now that she's decided she likes you, you have a friend for life."

Irdu and Autumn walked hand in hand, headed home. Their new apartment was only a few blocks from Liz and Marcus's house. It was small, but it had big, sunny windows, and best of all, the bedroom and the living room were separate rooms.

"I like her. I like that she's protective of you."

They lapsed into a comfortable silence. The sun continued to sink lower on the horizon.

"I have a gift for you," Irdu said suddenly.

"Again?"

Since he'd gotten his job at the library, he'd reveled in his ability to provide things to Autumn. He could rail against the tyranny of landlords in one breath, and then exclaim in delight over his ability to split rent with her on the next. He frequently came home with little oddities that he'd bought for her on a whim—an enameled keychain that looked like a paintbrush and palette, an elaborate chocolate truffle from a high-end chocolatier, a postcard-sized watercolor painting from a street artist, a tiny guillotine meant for cutting cigars, a bouquet of sunflowers, a ceramic cat that looked like the ones her grandmother had collected... the list went on.

"It's a gift for me, as well. Depending on your answer." He stopped and reached into his coat pocket. Autumn's heart thumped as he pulled a simple golden ring out. "Autumn, I love you. I waited a hundred lifetimes for you, and now that I have you, I never want to let you go. I have only myself to offer, but I offer you every last bit of me that I can give. Will you—"

"Yes!" Autumn threw her arms around him, eyes brimming with tears. "I would've married you the minute you became human. I would've married you when you were still a demon. I love you, and yes—*yes*—I will marry you!"

He kissed her and slid the band onto her ring finger.

"Let's get married right away," Autumn declared. "We'll go to the courthouse first thing tomorrow. Liz and Marcus can be our witnesses. I want a ring on your finger, too."

"Because I'm yours?" Irdu prompted with a smile.

"Because you're mine."

WHEN THEY GOT TO THEIR BUILDING, THEY BYPASSED their apartment and went up to the roof. Irdu had gotten into the habit of watching the sun rise and set every day. In the mornings, as soon as the first sliver of sunlight appeared over the horizon, he looked down at his hands, as if expecting to see himself dematerialize.

But he was still there. Every day. And every night. Autumn stood behind him as the sun sank lower, with her arms wrapped around his waist. She laid her ear against his back and listened to the whoosh of his breath, the thump of his heart.

He was real. And he was hers. Forever.

About the Author

Heather Guerre writes sexy-sweet fantasy, sci-fi, and contemporary romances. A hopeless romantic and an unapologetic nerd, Heather loves everything to do with romance, aliens, shifters, cyborgs, monsters, and magic.

For more from Heather, you can subscribe to her newsletter at heatherguerre.com/newsletter. Subscribers receive alerts for new releases as well as newsletter-exclusive bonus material.

FIND HEATHER ONLINE:

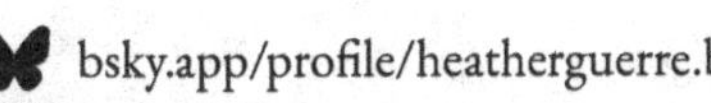

bsky.app/profile/heatherguerre.bsky.social

instagram.com/authorheatherguerre

goodreads.com/heatherguerre

bookbub.com/authors/heather-guerre

Thank You

Thank you for reading **Demon Lover!** If you enjoyed it (or even if you didn't), please consider reviewing or recommending it on social media and/or the retailer where you purchased it. Word of mouth has a huge impact on an author's success, and it helps other readers find new books to enjoy.

Also by Heather Guerre

Tooth & Claw series:

Paranormal Shifter and Vampire Romances

Cold Hearted

Hot Blooded

Once Bitten

—

Forbidden Mates series:

Sci-fi Alien Romances

Star Crossed

Moon Struck

Heart Song

—

Contemporary Romance:

Preferential Treatment